The

Wonderful Demise of
Benjamin Arnold Guppy

The
Wonderful Demise of
Benjamin Arnold Guppy

Gina Collia-Suzuki

Nezu Press

Published by Nezu Press

www.nezupress.com

First published 2008

© Gina Collia-Suzuki 2008

ISBN-13: 978-0-9559796-1-3

For Ryoma,
united we stand.

Gina Collia-Suzuki is a writer and artist who lives and works on the southwest coast of England, with her husband and a family of eight female rats. She does not spend her time contemplating ways of killing her neighbours... well, not much.

CHAPTER ONE

HAVE you ever wondered what it would be like to take the life of another human being? For most people that question goes unanswered. But I'm not one of those people. Not only am I part of that incredibly small group of private individuals who have extinguished the existence of another living soul, I am part of an even smaller minority in that I got away with it. I could go on right now to describe the events which took place immediately before, during, and after the demise of Ben Guppy, and to miss out no detail regarding his last breath and my part in it being his last. But to give a true picture of the man, and explain in some part the necessity for his death and my part in it, I will begin my story on the day our paths first crossed, on August 29th, 2003, when my husband Roy and I moved into our seaside flat at Hill View.

Guppy was standing in the shared driveway to our new home as we pulled up in our car, forced out to meet us by his relentless wife, Pat, to inspect the newcomers and discover if we were suitable neighbours. As it turned out, we were not. He made no effort to conceal his dislike of us from the outset, his opinion being formed immediately that we were not his sort of people. I consider myself fortunate in that. As we soon discovered, the individuals who frequented the Guppys' home so often proved to be cowards, liars, and thieves. But as I was saying, he was there in the driveway. His head was cocked to one side with that same lopsided grin and look of disapproval mixed with deluded superiority that seldom left his face for the next three years. I came to hate that expression of his. I often planned the method by which I would wipe it from his face. As it turned out, a broken neck did the trick.

Guppy was in his late seventies when we first met. There was nothing physically remarkable about him, unless being distinctly unattractive is considered remarkable. He was tall and thin, with very little hair and bad teeth. He fidgeted when forced to stand in one spot for more than five minutes, shifting his stance to place the weight of his body upon his right leg and then his left, often tugging at the seat of his trousers and bending his knees ever so slightly while he did so, in the manner of one frequently inflicted with a bout of haemorrhoids. He leaned in too close when he spoke, and held on for too long when he shook my hand.

The old man glanced over his shoulder to confirm that his wife was standing ready to assist him during this first encounter, in what turned out to be her usual position, concealed behind the front door to their ground floor flat, where she could be assured of a hasty escape, with or without her husband, from any conflict she inspired but was unwilling to see to its conclusion. The old man twitched, frowned, thrust both hands into his trouser pockets, puffed himself up, and opened his mouth to speak. He mumbled; his words barely audible. He paused, glanced back towards his conspicuously absent ally one more time, and began again. 'We go to bed at ten,' he said, pausing to await some confirmation from us that his message had been received and understood, 'except Sundays, when we prefer nine.' With that he turned to leave, appearing to feel that his mission had been accomplished. A few clicks emitted from the doorway to his home, however, made by an anxious wife with the aid of a door latch, alerted him to his error. He stopped dead and swung around. 'And dinner is at five.'

As he departed, we paused just long enough to readjust our mental facilities to digest this dialogue and conclude that it had been slightly unusual but also somewhat amusing, and then began making our way up the stone steps at the side of the building which led to our new home on the first floor. The significance of the information imparted by Ben Guppy eluded us until the clock struck five later that day. Three heavy knocks at the door, followed by four more in rapid succession, and the opening of our letterbox to enable the old man to examine the contents of our hallway, were followed by the sound of his voice calling out to confirm his presence and inform us that he was aware of ours. Within moments of the door being opened, the old man had barged past Roy, propelled himself along the hallway in the direction of our bathroom, and had begun investigating the contents of our bath.

'So it's tiles you're taking down,' he said, holding one up to support his statement and shaking it to emphasise his point. 'That's what all the noise is. Dinner is at five, I told you.'

Flinging the tile unceremoniously over his shoulder, and paying no attention to the sound of it skimming across the floor behind him, he then exited the room and marched along the hall in the direction of the front door, pushing me aside as he did so. As he neared the portal he halted. 'So no more noise, you hear,' he said, without pausing to receive a response. Then he was gone.

After once more taking a moment to process the old man's words, we concluded that, again, they had been unusual, but unlike our earlier encounter they had not been terribly amusing.

It is in the nature of all annoyingly happy young couples, however, to see the non-existent silver lining in every obviously deep grey rain cloud, so exclamations regarding the old man's rudeness were soon supplanted by optimistic reassurances regarding our soon-to-be harmonious coexistence within the building, once the old couple had come to know just how utterly nice we were.

So, what of Mrs Guppy? Well, she was no better than the old man. In fact, in many respects she was worse. I think I planned her downfall even more regularly than I did that of her husband. Perhaps, if the opportunity had presented itself, I might have done away with both of them. But by the time I was capable of the deed, she came out so rarely when I was about that I had to make do with offing just the one. I had never met a woman so thoroughly impressed with herself with so little reason to be. Shielded against the possibility of ever acquiring any brand of knowledge by a thick overcoat of ignorance, her lack of sense and intelligence went beyond mere common or garden stupidity. As to her physical appearance, she wore clothes that were too small, old and tired to contain her more than ample figure, and she was by far one of the most unattractive women I have ever had the misfortune to meet. With eyes narrowed and lips pursed, her facial features, appearing to have been formed as the result of sucking on copious quantities of bitter fruit, betrayed her sour and malicious character. And however often she did take a bath, it wasn't often enough. Indeed, as far as physical appearance and cleanliness were concerned, the Guppys were in every respect a matched pair.

The first time I met Pat Guppy she wore black. Black was her colour of choice when she meant business. And the business in question on that particular day, the second one in our new home, was the immediate termination of all renovation work within our flat. It's not that she asked us to stop. She didn't. No. She merely informed us of her status in the community, of her friendship with the Mayor and numerous council employees, and then insisted that we consider taking a break from decorating for our own benefit. Whilst making friends with the neighbours wasn't at the top of my list of priorities at that point, neither was making enemies. So I made an effort to be nice. She did not reciprocate.

'Your name's Alex then,' she said, adjusting the positioning of her glasses as she scrutinised me from top to bottom, and then from bottom to top. 'Funny sort of name for a woman.'

We hadn't invited her into our home. She'd entered through the front door, which had been left open while Roy took some garbage out of the flat. Most people knock, or ring the bell, or call out 'is anyone home' before crossing the threshold of a complete stranger's household. But Pat Guppy was not most people. Years of charity work and sitting on this board or the other had elevated her to such a level, in her own mind at least, that she transcended the boundaries of correct social behaviour that had been set in place to keep Joe Average in check. I was given, against my will, a complete and somewhat lengthy run down of everyone who had lived at the building before our arrival.

'We were here from the very beginning,' she said proudly. The beginning, she informed me, had been twelve years ago, and this had afforded them certain rights not enjoyed by other residents. She assured me that whilst things had not always run smoothly over the years, the Guppys had always been perfect neighbours and the other party in each and every case had been at fault.

'The Merediths were very unpleasant people,' she said, referring to the couple who had occupied our home before us. 'Eve Meredith always took her bath at eleven in the morning. Who in their right mind does that?'

The bubbles from said lady's bath had, she complained, been surplus to requirement, often making their way out of the drain and around to the Guppy's front step. No amount of complaining, and she insisted there had been a lot, had persuaded Mrs Meredith to desist and take her bath at a respectable hour, which was, according to the old woman, some time after eight in the evening. Those little alarm bells inside my head, the ones that are supposed to alert you when you're in the presence of a mad woman, should have been clanging away, but they were optimistically silent. The woman could talk and, rather like her verbose husband, she required no participation from me for the conversation to continue. She had a lot to say, and appeared to feel that she had very little time in which to say it. As it turned out, in that regard she was entirely correct. That first meeting was the only one of its kind, and after she left our home that day I never spoke a word to her again.

Whilst I had no difficulty in being downright ignorant if it saved me from more encounters with our nosey and decidedly odd neighbours, during those early days Roy felt some need to be sociable and to give the pair enough rope to hang themselves ten times over. The Guppys, who were the type of people who mistook friendliness and honesty for naivety and stupidity, saw Roy's willingness to accommodate them as a weakness in his character crying out to be exploited. So, during the first couple of weeks following our arrival at the property, Ben Guppy's visits to our home increased three-fold. Talking became complaining, and five minute chats became hour long reprimands. For my husband, a visit to the shops invariably included an encounter on the drive, instigated by the old man following a sprint from his property upon spotting Roy out of doors. A trip to the dustbin was followed by a chance meeting by the rhododendrons, during which suggestions would be made regarding the volume of our television, or the hour at which a man should leave for work, as half past five in the morning was terribly inconvenient and inconsiderate. The Guppys were always up by half past five, the old man had said, but they were concerned that, had they been asleep when Roy left for work, they would surely have been woken.

By the end of the second fortnight, we had a very complete idea of the old pair's daily schedule; not because we had any interest in their comings and goings, but because Ben Guppy had been very eager from the outset to inform us of their every movement. At ten o'clock in the morning on Mondays and Thursdays, except during a bank holiday, Pat Guppy apparently entertained extremely important members of an immensely influential branch of the local government. On Fridays, at two o'clock in the afternoon, she took calls from the Prime Minister, who was always eager to hear what she had to say about the running of our country. Sundays were for church-going and gardening, and evenings were for banquets with high ranking members of the local constabulary. Between those times, the old woman could be found in various locations around the town, which were apparently very lucky to have her, doing charitable works. Such works, as we later discovered, included facilitating the supply of narcotics to local addicts, and collecting regular payments from councillors who had been overly amorous with their secretarial help but considerably less discreet.

The frequent updates which, we were told, should have been added to our calendar to avoid misunderstandings, came to an abrupt halt on November 9th 2003, which was a Sunday. The customary church-going and gardening had been replaced by a party to which, the old man had asserted, only the *crème de la crème* of local society had been invited. Judging by the fact that no human being apart from the old man and his wife had entered or exited the building during that day, Roy and I concluded that the visitor list must have been incredibly short, but the lack of tangible living guests did not dissuade Ben Guppy from referring at great length to the discomfort afforded those individuals as a result of the noise which emanated from our flat at half past three that afternoon. This particular complaint was not outstanding due to the ferocity of its delivery, but rather the location of it.

Having plugged a small hand-held sander into the mains only five minutes previously, Roy was busy removing old plaster from beneath the window frame in our living room while I scraped away at ageing wallpaper atop an extended ladder when the sound of what appeared to be fists hammering against the exterior of the living room door filled the air. All activity ceased. We stood perfectly still, and perfectly silent, awaiting a repeat performance to confirm the source of the sound. Bang, bang, bang. The door shook on its hinges as the pounding continued. Bang, bang, bang, bang. The pounding came again; quicker this time. Rubber mallet in hand, Roy approached the door and reached out to turn its knob. In one fluid movement he opened the door and retreated back into the room, to place some distance between himself and the stranger who had been so eager to make his presence known.

'Twenty minutes I've spent trying to get you on the telephone,' Ben Guppy exclaimed, 'don't you ever answer your 'phone?'

Roy did not speak. The element of surprise does wonders when it comes to silencing the average human being. The remarks which come to mind so quickly with the benefit of hindsight are distinctly absent when we encounter the unimaginable or the unexplainable. The old man shook visibly, unable to control the anger he was experiencing as a result of the perceived inconsiderate unwillingness on our part to take his call. He repeated his question.

'How did you...?" Roy began.

'You left the door open.'

The fact that this claim could not have been true washed over us, but as I descended the ladder I had been firmly gripping onto since the old man had made his appearance, the sound of movement, as the metal steps creaked beneath my weight, gave Roy the jolt necessary to bring him to his senses. Moving forward at speed, he took Ben Guppy by the arm and began pushing him backwards, out of the doorway and into the hall.

'The noise,' Guppy said, attempting to brush off Roy's hold on him, 'it's terribly inconvenient. We have guests.'

'Get out!' Roy bellowed. 'Get out now!'

The two men grappled with each other as they moved along the narrow passageway, bumping up against a slim walnut table as they approached the entrance vestibule. As the old man was forced in the direction of the front doorway he reached out and grabbed at the door frame, attempting to delay his ejection, and tugged at Roy's t-shirt to maintain his hold before being pushed unceremoniously out into the open air. As Roy attempted to close the front door, the old man lunged forward. Forcing one foot in between the door and its frame, he called out 'I want to talk to you'. Then, as the slamming of wood against the side of his shoe forced him to recoil in pain, allowing Roy the opportunity to seal the portal once and for all, the old man shouted 'Let me in! I'll have you!'

Being thrown out with a flea in his ear did not deter Ben Guppy from continuing to attempt a dialogue. Beating his fists against the slightly distorted glazed panels set into the upper half of the solid wooden door which barred his entrance, the old man cursed and swore for ten full minutes before running out of steam. Then, after having been called down to the driveway by his overly excited wife for a cup of strong sweet tea to keep him going, he returned to his former position and the pounding began again. The effects of the tea lasted all of fifteen minutes and then, after giving the door frame one last wallop, which coincided with a loud yelp and severe complaining about the sharp pain in his wrist, old man Guppy withdrew. Half an hour later, following a loud argument within the Guppy's flat below, most of which was entirely audible, the old man once more made his way to the tiled surface immediately outside our home, raised the flap of the letterbox, and shoved a sealed envelope through it with some force. The first of his notes had arrived.

'Dear Mr and Mrs Leah,' the note began. 'My wife and I are sorely disappointed by your unprovoked attack upon my person, which seems to have dislodged something painful and may require a visit to the doctor's surgery in the morrow. Our guests, comprising briefly the Mayor, his wife, three local members of Her Majesty's parliament, several members of the local history society, and the vicar, were all too upset to stay beyond hors d'oeuvres and canapés, so my wife going to the trouble of making a sherry trifle was all for nothing. We shall be lodging a formal complaint with the Environmental Health Department concerning this matter and have alerted the local branch of Neighbourhood Watch additionally. I will forward the doctor's bill when it is received. Yours Sincerely, Mr Benjamin Arnold Guppy, Esquire.'

Despite the events which occurred during that Sunday afternoon, old man Guppy continued to try to waylay Roy and I whenever he happened to bump into us on the driveway or in the street. When I say 'happened to bump into', I am in fact referring to those times when, having heard our front door open, or the sound of footfalls on the stone steps leading down from our flat, the old man would exit his home at high speed and make a mad dash along the tarmac until he caught up with his target. Having been ignored completely for all of two weeks, Guppy's tactics changed and, in addition to sprinting out of his flat and hurling himself in our direction whenever he caught our scent, the old man began positioning himself between Roy or myself and our car whenever we returned from the supermarket, so that it became impossible to remove shopping from the boot without first removing him. 'Iceland's peas are cheaper,' he'd say, examining the contents of our Tesco carrier bags before being nudged aside. 'Now what are you going to do about the state of your garden? Your hedge has grown so tall that my wife can no longer see through number two's windows without using a step ladder.'

Having been overcome by a brief spell of new-home insanity during our first couple of days at the property, Roy had been persuaded, by an anxious Ben Guppy who spouted tales of leaking pipes and exploding ovens, to give the old man our unlisted telephone number, in case of emergencies. I suppose the word 'emergency' is open to interpretation to a certain extent, but it did not occur to either one of us that it could encompass a reminder to close our curtains after dark, a request that we pick up a discarded newspaper from beside our car as it was causing an obstruction, or a complaint about the amount of walking about we did just outside our own home, which apparently made Pat Guppy feel uneasy and somewhat harassed. If anyone called on us while we were out, we received a call to let us know, which invariably included a blow by blow account of the number of knocks on the door or rings on the bell, the length of time spent waiting for an answer which did not come, and the general demeanor of the caller following the realisation that their visit had been fruitless. A brief encounter on the drive, during which Roy may have made some reference to wringing the old man's scrawny neck, resulted in four days of complete telephonic silence. Then... ring ring, ring ring.

'Come! Come quickly! Water everywhere!' the old man exclaimed.

Whatever our feelings may have been towards the elderly couple, and mine were becoming increasingly hostile, although not at all homicidal, and in spite of the fact that the call had come at half past four in the morning, the sound of panic in Ben Guppy's voice coupled with the knowledge that several pipes in our bathroom had been worked on by a plumber the evening before, sent Roy running out of the front door and down the stone steps to the drive, half-dressed and out of breath but ready for action. Ben Guppy was awaiting his arrival at the entrance to his dilapidated domicile, fully dressed and entirely composed.

'If you'll come this way,' he said calmly, moving aside so that Roy could make his way inside. 'The spare bedroom is along the hall and to the left.' Coming up from behind, as Roy followed the old man's directions and arrived at the rear of the flat, where the door to one of the old couple's bedrooms stood wide open, Ben Guppy continued: 'I tried to mop up the water with a sponge, and it seems to have stopped coming through now, but it's ruined the paintwork as you can see.' The old man gestured upwards, pointing out a small patch, of about six inches in diameter, where a brown stain was situated on the ceiling alongside the ornate plaster cornicing. 'The entire ceiling will need to be repainted.'

'He'd do it himself,' Pat Guppy chimed in, 'but he can't get up a ladder.'

The old man nodded, an expression of mock sincerity creeping across his face. 'Not since my brain surgery,' he said.

It's a funny thing, the way a simple statement can inspire such a feeling of pity, even without the provision of concrete proof to support it, that the most sensible of people will fall under its spell. Roy fixed his gaze upon the thin old man who, swaying gently like a palm tree in a soft breeze, looked to be one banana short of a full bunch, and empathised just long enough to utter the words 'I'll have a painter come and give me a quote for the work.'

Secure in the belief that their deceit had harnessed a new money horse for them, the Guppys, already salivating, ushered Roy out of their home with smiling faces and promises of neighbourly coffee mornings and the swapping of gardening tips during warm summer afternoons. Before saying his farewells, Ben Guppy insisted on shaking hands three times to seal the deal, pointing out in a cautionary manner that a gentleman's word was his bond, which seemed to imply that he had perceived in Roy's character a certain sense of duty and honour which was sorely lacking in his own. Pat Guppy pointed out, thrice and at great length, that she was connected to all the right people and frequented all the right places, and offered to put in a good word for us, to elevate us in the eyes of our neighbours, whilst at the same time highlighting her ability to affect a change in the opposite direction.

The old woman's offer of assistance in this regard was ironic, as she and her husband had done everything in their power, during the preceding weeks, to inspire in our neighbours a mounting suspicion regarding our background, a great deal of doubt regarding our honesty, and a belief that we were, if pushed, capable of doing away with elderly folk as they slept quietly in their beds. Admittedly, the latter claim turned out to be correct in part where I was concerned, but at the time these rumours first began circulating I had no desire to choke the life out of anyone. By the time we hit the three month anniversary of our move to the building, all but a handful of our neighbours were refusing to give us the time of day, having chosen their side of the fence, and the few who were willing to exchange pleasantries were nonetheless of the opinion that, as there can never be copious amounts of smoke without a pretty big fire, we must have done something to inspire the Guppys' accusations.

Pat Guppy believed that she was admired and respected by all who were deemed worthy of her condescension. In truth she was feared and disliked. When Pat Guppy spoke everyone listened, not just because she was known to have connections in both high and low places, and had demonstrated on numerous occasions previously that she was more than willing to call on the latter group in times of need, but because she was absurd. A malformed, physically unappealing lump of a woman, possessed of the intelligence and personality of a wet sock, she was both repulsive and fascinating at the same time, and for the same reason: that she had bullied, provoked, chastised, badgered and slandered her way to where she was, and that for all her effort she was no better off than most, and considerably worse off than many. She claimed a large and faithful following, but whilst it was true that a great number of people would indeed rush to the Guppys' front door with gusto, to hear the latest news with regards to the old pair's various dirty tricks campaigns, they were compelled to do so largely due to the hope that one day the news would be bad and would involve numerous backfires and some tragic, and by that I mean poetically just, outcome for the old couple. The guppys were a permanent crash site, monitored by a troupe of faithful and persistent rubber neckers.

Our home was situated within a building which housed four flats in total. In addition to ours, and the Guppys' shabby abode, there were two flats at basement level, one owned by Anne and Dave Roper, a couple of approximately the same age as ourselves, and the other inhabited by a somewhat older man by the name of James Floyd. The first time we met Dave Roper he told us that, just prior to our arrival, he and his wife had been the focus of the old pair's attention. They had gone through the same sequence of events which we'd experienced, albeit over a considerably more protracted period of time, including several attempts by the old man to break into their home, two of which had been successful. They had, however, chosen to remain on speaking terms with the Guppys because they felt, as many do in these situations, that there is an obligation to make every effort to get along with your neighbours and to make allowances when dealing with people of a certain age. Dave Roper expressed his unbridled delight concerning our arrival at the property, as the old pair had shifted the focus of their malicious attention immediately to us and were subsequently leaving both him and his wife alone entirely. He was incredibly grateful to us for making his life so much better, and not at all sorry that it had been to our detriment, as the latter had been necessary to bring about the former.

'All we had for months was that old git knocking on our door. The TV was too loud, we were slamming the doors too much, our vacuum cleaner was irritating, we used the shower too early in the morning,' Dave Roper said. 'One thing after another. We thought it would never stop.' He paused to reflect and then grinned. 'Then you came along,' he continued, 'and all our problems were over.' He grinned again. A suggestion from Roy that we should band together to put the Guppys in their place once and for all removed that grin. 'Oh no,' Dave said, 'we'd not be up for anything like that.'

With that he turned and was about to head away from us when he stopped, stepped closer, leaned in, looked around conspiratorially to check that there were no ears flapping in the bushes, and said quietly 'they have keys to all the flats, you know that right?'

The expression of utter shock on my face, coupled with escalating anger on Roy's, alerted Dave Roper to the fact that we had not been privy to this piece of information prior to that conversation, so he went on. 'The old bloke who lived in your place before the Merediths gave them a key to your place, daft old bugger. Nice bloke though, he was. Don't know how they got their hands on the rest of them.' He pushed his hands deep into his pockets and shrugged, half smiled, lowered his eyes, checked that the coast was clear, and then retreated. 'It's not personal though,' he said, as he reached his garden gate and was about to enter safe territory, 'they hate everyone.' And with that he was gone.

It wasn't personal. That was true at the beginning. The Guppys had been used to getting what they wanted, but had never had any real interest in the people they were getting it from. Their inquisitive behaviour during the early days was not fuelled by some desire to know us better with a view to improving relations between our two households. No. It was a means to an end, for how can you hope to defeat your enemy if you do not know him? Every single person who had come up against the malicious old pair, until our arrival at Hill View, had given them whatever they asked for, whenever they asked for it. They were entirely unaccustomed to the word 'no.' Their methods had been tried and tested over numerous years, and a long list of conquests testified to the fact that they were bound to succeed and we were bound to fail. Or, at least, that was the way it was supposed to play out. Had it done so, the Guppys would have taken us to the cleaners and then, with insincere smiles plastered across their worn faces, uttered the pathetically consolatory words 'no hard feelings.' They would have gone on living beneath us, happy in the knowledge that we were owned. But that is not the way it played out.

When old man Guppy came calling later that day, wanting to know where the painter had got to who was supposed to be painting his damaged ceiling, following the downpour of water which had gone on for two hours, according to him, but had nonetheless left nothing more than a dry stain no bigger than a sandwich plate, the door was slammed firmly in his face. When a note arrived, asking after the same tradesman, it was filed and forgotten. And when Ben Guppy, having realised that neither doorstep inquiries nor written entreaties would achieve the desired result, made a mad dash along the drive in Roy's direction and called out 'I'd do it myself, but I'm no good with a ladder,' he met with nothing but a cold stare and silence. 'We shook on it, God damn you!' he called out. Again, silence.

But what of the old man's penchant for a spot of breaking and entering, and Dave Roper's claim that the old pair had been in possession of keys to each flat long before our arrival? Only an hour and a half after that discussion had taken place, a jolly chap from 'A Lock of Hair' was on our doorstep. The business, which occupied two floors in the centre of town, was run by the cheerful middle-aged gentleman in question, one Brian Wellgood, expert in the field of door fixings, and his dear wife Noreen Wellgood, hairdresser to the over sixties, and between the two of them they claimed the odd distinction of being able to change your locks and curl them at the same time. Whilst the Guppys were away for the evening, most likely shafting a local councillor at a banquet for morally corrupt social climbers, the lock to our front door, which had apparently been very familiar with a key kept about old man Guppy's person, was discarded.

During the following couple of days there was a lot of shouting on Ben Guppy's part, and an even greater amount of silence on ours. Our comings and goings were monitored, noted down with times attached, commented on, criticised, and broadcast to the neighbours. Small assemblies began to form at the entrance to our driveway, peopled by elderly men and women who were almost as disagreeable in physical appearance as the Guppys themselves but, remarkably as it hardly seemed possible, considerably less educated if their loud dialogues, accompanied by highly animated gesticulations and hammed up gasps, were any indication of their collective level of intelligence. Pat Guppy attended each and every gathering, usually in possession of a clipboard and pen, which she appeared to believe gave her a certain air of officialdom. Her husband, with red face and clenched fists, presented his evidence for the prosecution, which included several notes sent to us by the old man which he, as he pointed out whilst casting his gaze in an accusatory manner towards the pavement where garbage bags were left every Monday morning for collection, had been forced to fish out from our rubbish after we had discarded them without making any response. All assembled would sigh as they contemplated the unquestionably inconsiderate nature of every member of the younger generation, for whom they had fought so bravely during the war, despite having been only ten years old at the time. Pat Guppy would shed a crocodile tear, one or more of the congregation would pat her on the back, to acknowledge her stoic resilience in the face of such horrifying treatment, and the jury would return its verdict. It was a unanimous decision; we were guilty as charged. Suspicions were aired regarding our background and motives, with the general consensus of opinion being that we were in the business of driving the elderly mad, and as the end of that particular week approached, we were elevated from the level of common or garden petty criminals with dodgy relatives in the East End to well-connected drug dealers with family spread out across Colombia.

It was the fifth day in December, which was a Friday, at about one o'clock in the afternoon, when the carpet fitters arrived to provide a soft woollen covering for our living room floor. The old carpet was torn up and disposed of in a matter of minutes. The hardboard was cut, positioned, and pinned to the floorboards by means of countless small nails in about half an hour, and by four o'clock we were positioning the sofa and preparing to manoeuvre a very tall, and very heavy, display cabinet. The doorbell, which had been fixed the previous day, rang as we began searching the surfaces of the large piece of furniture, attempting to locate a position which would facilitate a firm grip. As my mother had been due to arrive at around that time, we did not experience the usual sense of apprehension which had, by that point, accompanied every knock at the portal. Roy opened the door in a very cheerful manner, expecting to welcome her inside. The face which greeted him, however, was not that of my mother. Ben Guppy, with features more contorted than usual, stood outside, slightly hunched and half soaked as the light winter drizzle had turned into a downpour somewhere between his own front door and ours. Amid the anger and obvious vexation, there was a smug grin just breaking out on the old man's face.

Ben Guppy recounted the story of how he and his dear elderly wife had been sitting in their living room that afternoon, and had watched pictures fly from their walls and ornaments dance off the sides of mantelpieces. The old man had, apparently, sat and watched his chandelier swing to the left and to the right, then left and right again, to the beat of the carpet layer's hammer. With much embellishment, he went on to describe his mounting distress, and that of the old woman, and their ultimate decision to vacate their home due to the noise making its way down from above.

'We feared the ceiling would fall in and crush us,' the old man said, raising his eyes to the sky and his hands to his face to illustrate the sense of dread he was attempting to convey. 'My wife had one of her turns, and we almost went to the hospital to have my brain scanned. Anyway, the Palmers next door took us in for an hour until your fitters left.'

They had moved all ornaments and pictures from their living room before going, the old man went on to explain, for fear that their precious and highly valuable family heirlooms would be hurled onto the ground and smashed into small pieces. 'They are irreplaceable,' Ben Guppy said, 'worth tens of pounds.' He then described how, after much swinging, juddering, and jangling about, the chandelier had detached itself from the ceiling and fallen to the ground, fracturing one limb as it bounced off the coffee table and ricocheted into the fireplace. 'It swung this way and that,' he repeated, 'until it came crashing down with a frightful noise and scared us both half to death.'

'So you were at home when the chandelier fell?' Roy asked, calmly.

The old man nodded excitedly.

'But you were out, because of the noise?'

There was a brief silence.

'Ah, well, now you see...' the old man began, rubbing his hands together and losing his smug grin for a nanosecond before regaining his composure. He raised his hand triumphantly, having just conceived of a response which he thought would go some way in extricating himself from the hole he'd just dug. 'We came back!' he exclaimed in a self-congratulatory manner. 'Yes, we came back.' He sighed, then licked his lips. 'We did,' he concluded. Then, as he finished off his elaborate tale with the brief mention that, having just sat down to afternoon tea as the cacophony first assaulted their ears, his wife had spilled a spot onto her favourite doyley and left an irremovable stain, he reached the main business of the day. He ceremoniously presented Roy with a bill for eighty pounds which would, he claimed, cover the cost of a replacement light fitting from John Lewis' department store. 'There will be the expense of an accredited electrical engineer, of course, so that bill will follow.'

And there it was, the reason for the old man's smug grin. That look of arrogantly confident expectation on the old man's face was due to the fact that not for a single moment had he or his wife considered the possibility that we would turn him away. They had been so sure of their own entitlement and of our stupidity, possibly fuelled by the belief that we were going to get around to paying for their ceiling to be painted eventually, that they had already made preparations for a visit to their store of choice, and while Ben Guppy stood before Roy, perpetrating an act of fraud, Pat Guppy sat in the couple's car, which was sitting in the driveway with its engine running, ready to go shopping. She looked expectantly in her husband's direction, awaiting visual confirmation that their plan was a go.

'Even if we did accept responsibility for your broken light,' Roy said, observing the old woman as she opened the car door and prepared to exit it to find out what was causing the delay, 'we're not going to just hand over eighty quid here and now.'

The old man's shoulders sank. He sighed, shook his head, looked to his wife for support, and then spoke.

'Look here,' he said, attempting an air of reasonable persuasiveness, 'I'm not as young as I used to be.' His shoulders fell further and he developed a stoop. He put one hand to his lower back and moved forward one faux-hobbled step. 'We have to live off a meagre pension and we just about make ends meet. We have a broken light sitting downstairs that needs replacing, and you obviously have the money to pay for it.' He paused. Then, noting the lack of sympathy being displayed by my husband, Ben Guppy's posture shifted, his back straightened, he clenched his fist and raised it to within an inch of Roy's face. 'So give me the fucking money!' he screamed.

Once again Ben Guppy stood upon the wet tiles outside our home, barred from entering by the part-glazed wooden door that had been slammed shut a fraction of an inch from the end of his nose. The pounding began about fifteen seconds later, accompanied by the old man's cries that we should open up immediately and let him in. A sudden downpour, however, forced him down the stone steps and back to his car, the doors of which had been left wide open by his wife as she fled the scene when the rain began to fall. He slammed the passenger door shut, cursing as he did so, and then rushed around to the other side of the car and climbed into the driver's seat. The sound of the gear stick grating as it was forced into position without the complete co-operation of the clutch filled the damp air. The engine screamed as the old man forced his foot down on the accelerator. Then, as the clutch was released, the car jerked backwards at speed only to come to an abrupt halt just prior to making contact with our garden wall. The car stood motionless for a moment. Then, as the grating and grinding began again, it bunny-hopped along the drive, stalled, started up again, stalled once more, and finally rolled down the incline at the edge of the drive and made its way onto the street and out of sight.

Later in the evening, as we left our home to make a visit to the local supermarket, we slowed the car as we passed by the front of the Guppys' home. The contents of the old pair's living room were clearly visible through the large bay window which fronted it, across which the curtains were never drawn so as to permit mere mortals who happened to be passing to see how the other, more superior, half lived. It was not simply the lack of curtain cover, however, which afforded a clear view into the Guppys' home. It was the presence of a fully functioning, entirely attached, completely intact and highly illuminating chandelier. Pat Guppy was positioned in her usual spot close by the window, and was holding an open book with which to affect the illusion of being engaged in reading rather than monitoring the traffic and passers-by. The sound of our car leaving the drive had alerted her to the presence of a vehicle nearby, but it was not until we were in plain sight that she was able to identify its occupants. As we came to a stop opposite the old couple's home, the old woman sprung into action, flinging her book over her shoulder as she thrust her hands up into the air and began signalling to her husband. The old man, who had not been visible until he shot bolt upright from his chair at the behest of his wife, made his way to the back of the room and then, along with the old woman, disappeared from sight as the room fell into darkness.

The following day, as Roy prepared to leave for work and placed his briefcase and suit jacket inside our car, Pat Guppy approached him. She made a great show of being a reasonable human being and apologised for her husband's behaviour. She said that she hoped he hadn't given us too hard a time, but insisted we would have no choice but to forgive them both when we heard what an awfully bad week they'd suffered. She was all false smiles and declarations of genuine friendship. She referred to olive branches and her desire to offer several of them under the right circumstances. And then she outlined her terms.

'He's an old man,' she said, 'and he's not been the same since his stroke.' She scanned Roy's face and awaited the customary display of charitable concern. 'He can't climb a ladder so an electrician will have to be called out. More cost, you see? He gets a bee in his bonnet and away he goes, but surely you won't hold that against me. I've done you no wrong. Come now.' She moved closer, reaching out with one hand to touch Roy's sleeve.

'Talk to your insurance company,' Roy said coldly, 'we want nothing more to do with you.'

'You won't pay?' Pat Guppy asked, with a feigned look of surprise. Then she smiled. 'Oh I think you will. People around here are already beginning to ask me how our new neighbours are settling in. They want to know if we're being treated well you see. And we certainly wouldn't want to go giving you a bad reputation.' Her voice was calm and measured, and she smiled as she spoke. 'Our acquaintances in the local area are immensely influential.'

She went on to say that her powers of influence were not restricted to those in high office, and that if the need arose she was perfectly prepared to enlist the help of friends who operated outside of the law and without conscience. Scanning Roy's face, and seeing not a single sign that his resolve was weakening, she cocked her head to one side and pursed her lips. 'So it's like that?'

And with that the battle lines were drawn up.

CHAPTER TWO

S O, do I sound like a homicidal maniac yet? No? Well, that will be because I wasn't yet entertaining the idea of murdering my neighbours and, to be fair, I don't think my senses have ever deteriorated to the point where the label 'maniac' could be applied. The term does suggest a certain level of mental instability, which I know did not exist at the time of Ben Guppy's death or during the period prior to it. I wouldn't want anyone to get the wrong idea here. I don't intend, at any point, to whip out that particular 'get out of jail free' card and claim temporary insanity.

And speaking of insanity, by the time we decorated our Christmas tree, at the beginning of the second week of December, I did consider our elderly neighbours to be quite mad. I couldn't conceive of any rational reason for their behaviour towards us, and came rather hastily to the conclusion that the old pair must have lost their senses entirely. Of course, they were no more insane than I was at that point, and there was a reason for everything that had taken place up until that point and everything that was yet to unfold. People lie for it, cheat for it, and they often murder for it. Money.

My belief that they were thoroughly unhinged, however, was reinforced by the notes that were finding their way through our letterbox with increased frequency. Told, in no uncertain terms, that we would not enter into any discussion with them again, their need to maintain some form of dialogue forced them in the direction of the written word. One note dropped onto our doormat the night following Pat Guppy's declaration of war, and contained her husband's assertions concerning our culpability with regards to his broken chandelier. It was typed, and included a demand for eighty pounds. The next to arrive, which was also typed, echoed its predecessor, as did the two which followed shortly after. And following their arrival, one note arrived each and every evening, at about half past seven, for the next couple of weeks. The old man would slowly and quietly ascend the stone steps to our flat, in an attempt to reach our front door undetected, and after pushing the note through the letterbox, as silently as possible, he would descend the steps at great speed and dash into his flat before slamming his front door loudly with all his might. Amid the requests for money, the odd complaint was still to be found regarding the slamming of doors, the usage of a washing machine after dinner, or the positioning of garbage bags on the pavement outside in an asymmetrical manner, causing the frontage of the property to look common. Generally, one or all of these things caused so much distress to the old woman that she was forced to have one of her pills, and the old man, if he were to be believed, became a frequent visitor to the local hospital, where he would be submitted to an emergency CAT scan.

As the days passed, and the number of notes received went into double and then triple figures, the old man's neatly written productions on clean white paper deteriorated into scrawled, almost incoherent demands on crumpled bright yellow post-it notes. The fact that we did not reply did not seem to deter the old couple. In fact, as the number of ignored communications increased so too did their desire to conjure up yet another, along with the old man's desire to observe what went on inside our home. Rather than speeding off down the steps in the direction of his home after dropping off his latest scribbled production, he took to loitering outside our front door for ten minutes or more, with his nose pressed firmly against the glass, trying to catch a glimpse of some activity within or hear some portion of a private conversation.

Telling Ben Guppy to bugger off did not work. Nor did threatening to sock him on the nose if he didn't. Attempting a removal by force resulted in him screaming 'assault' at the top of his voice, bringing out Mrs Palmer from next door, who assured us that she would be more than willing to act as a witness on the old man's behalf if the police were called. So, five days before Christmas, a carpenter was brought in; a carpenter with a very heavy, very solid, and entirely unglazed replacement front door. He arrived first thing in the morning and parked his white van on the drive at the foot of the frost-covered stone steps that led to our home. The sound of an unfamiliar vehicle pulling up outside had the Guppys rushing out to observe the event, and when the visitor's purpose was exposed, as the rear doors of his vehicle were flung open to reveal its woody contents, the old man called out for a pen and paper to take notes and then rushed to his garage to get out his car.

Ben Guppy drove up and down the shared driveway repeatedly as the old door was being removed from its hinges. He went back and forth, forth and back, pausing only to roll down his window, look up at our portal with sheer disgust, and cuss loudly. 'You need planning permission for that!' he called out frustratedly, and every so often he would get out of his car and produce a camera, to take a souvenir shot of the old door being manoeuvred down the stone steps, or the new one being carried up them. He also photographed the carpenter, and the carpenter's van. And when this didn't inspire the cessation of works, he got out of his car, dashed across the drive, and screamed 'bastards!' at the top of his lungs.

'I'm 'phoning the Mayor!' Pat Guppy called out, positioning herself in the centre of the drive to avoid going unnoticed. She thrust one arm into the air and began waving a cordless telephone about to add weight to her threat. 'Mr Mayor,' she exclaimed into the handset, before dialling, 'it's your dear friend Pat Guppy here.'

The one-sided conversation went on, and included an explanation about the removal of a single domestic front door, prior to being granted consent by the council's planning department and her good self, the discomfort inflicted by us upon two elderly and defenceless, though highly valued and respected, members of the local community, and a point blank refusal to run for government office regardless of the encouragement she had received, on too many occasions to count, from members of the Royal household. She waved the handset once more, triumphantly. The carpenter laughed out loud. Ben Guppy rushed forward and whipped out his camera. The carpenter laughed again.

The old man's camera made numerous appearances over the coming few weeks. At first he photographed our front door. Then he photographed the painter painting the front door, and the paint with which he was painting it. And following the painter's departure he moved on to taking snap shots of our windows. Initially, whilst his happy snapping could still be explained away as the result of some desire to accurately record the condition of the building, he stood in full view in the driveway with his camera poised for action. Then, when inanimate objects lost their appeal and the need for discretion increased, he moved his operation to the street that ran alongside the building and positioned himself behind our garden wall, in a spot where he could be partially obscured by the lilac tree that grew nearby, and waited for one or both of us to appear. Snap snap went the old man's camera, as we were immortalised in the act of opening a door, walking, carrying shopping, or taking out a bag of rubbish. A few odd remarks from men and women out walking their dogs, or traversing the street to post a letter, however, forced the old man back onto the property, to a less advantageous but considerably more concealed location.

To the rear of the building in which we lived stood two dilapidated garages, one belonging to ourselves and the other to the Guppys. Nearby a small patch of land, overgrown with weeds and containing an old white plastic table and an even older wooden bench, served as a garden for the old pair. So, did they use this area for outdoor dining, or the occasional cocktail on a balmy summer evening? Did they cultivate roses there, or sit reading the paper on Sunday morning? No. Fronted by a patchwork of latticed panels, the surfaces of which were thickly covered with climbing plants during the summer and autumn, the primary function of that little corner of the world was to serve as a lookout post for the old man, and occasionally his wife too, to enable either one of them to observe and note down the comings and goings of all who lived nearby. From their moss-covered wooden bench, through strategically cultivated gaps in the growth which covered the rickety trellis, they were perfectly situated during the warmer weather to keep an eye on anyone arriving at the property or leaving it, and they were even better placed to monitor activity within our kitchen or study. But we were in the dead of winter. The golden glow of autumn had slipped away, taking with it ninety percent of the old pair's leafy partition.

Nevertheless the old man, oblivious to the loss of cover, took up his position each day behind the few random branches that remained, to observe our kitchen window for ten to twenty minutes at a time, happily snapping away at anything that moved. And this activity continued throughout the Christmas period, into the New Year of 2004, through January and February, and well into March. The routine varied only minimally from one day to the next, always beginning with ten minutes' observation at the front of the property, and then five beside the lilac tree, followed by a lengthy stint at the rear, behind the thin covering of brittle twigs. Every so often Pat Guppy would join her husband and the old pair would surveil the building together, but generally speaking the old woman lasted only a matter of moments before returning indoors.

'I'd stay out here with you,' the old woman would call out, as she left her husband shivering on the damp wooden seat, 'but you know how I suffer with my knees.'

On very rare occasions the old pair would sit within the lookout post in the rain, sharing a flask of tea and a packed luncheon, but such activity usually coincided with the arrival of new furniture to our home or the delivery of a large parcel. The latter annoyed both the old man and his wife immensely because, whereas a large piece of furniture was usually clearly visible and almost certainly identifiable by its shape, there was no way to discern the contents of a package without opening it up and examining it personally. Having discovered that return address labels do not provide much assistance when trying to discover the contents of your neighbour's mail, after rescuing large amounts of discarded brown paper from black refuse sacks filled with rotting vegetables, the Guppys suffered a great amount of vexation each time goods arrived through the post. The unfortunate soul who delivered such items was followed, observed, and then questioned if he did not manage to escape before the old man caught up with him. Regular callers knew to wear running shoes and park close by, but one-off callers were invariably snared before they could reach the safety of their vehicle.

It's odd, the things we humans can become accustomed to, and even find comfort in. After three months of each day being little altered from the one before, we became complacent and dismissive. By the middle of March we had resigned ourselves to the fact that we would most likely be the subject of the old pair's attentions until they sold up and moved or dropped down dead. We wrongly assumed, as the old pair had not deviated from their routine to any great extent for so many weeks, preferring to watch from a safe distance rather than attempt any direct contact with us, that they would continue in the same fashion and that living with them would offer no great surprises from that point forward. We considered the situation to be manageable, and began to feel comfortable.

We were entirely unprepared, therefore, when the first note in almost three months landed on our doormat at half past one on a Monday afternoon during the third week of March. I'd spent the morning in the bedroom, atop a long ladder, scraping at old encrusted wallpaper. From my high vantage point I had a clear view of Pat Guppy as she stood beside the old couple's small car, which was parked on the street alongside the building in what had, by then, become its usual daytime location. She was gesturing wildly to her husband, who was at that point out of sight. I heard the letterbox open and close, the sound of footsteps making their way from the first floor to ground level, and saw Ben Guppy appear on the drive as he made his way towards its exit. He turned right, walked along the path beside our garden wall, and headed towards his wife as she made ready to climb inside their vehicle. 'That will sort them out,' he called out to her, smiling smugly and congratulating himself on a job well done. Within moments the engine started up, and the old pair were soon making their getaway at speed. Their excitement was readily discernible, so I assumed that the note would contain either a complaint about noise or a demand for financial compensation. It contained both.

'Dear Mr and Mrs Leah,' the old man had scrawled at the top of the shabby sheet of discoloured paper. 'There is water pouring through the ceiling of our bedroom and running down the curtains. The ceiling will need to be made good and painted, the curtains will need to be replaced, and the carpet has shrunk so that will have to go too. Mr Axley from across the road came over to witness the damage so we trust you'll take your responsibilities more seriously this time. I am referring here to the repainting of the ceiling in our spare bedroom which is outstanding and the eighty pounds still owed. Also, you played your gramophone records twice yesterday and caused so much distress that we suffered terrible pains in our heads and my wife insisted I go to bed with her. If you are planning to do it again please consult with us to arrange a convenient time. Tomorrow we will be out between ten in the morning and midday, so we have no objection to you playing them then.'

A second note followed just a few days later, as the water began pouring into their home from a different location in the same room, soaking their duvet and mattress. A third note had puddles appearing on their kitchen ceiling, some forty or so feet away from the original spot, and by the fourth note, which arrived one day later, the water had moved back to the bedroom and had destroyed Pat Guppy's dressing table and a photograph of her dear mother.

Following the delivery of a fifth note, Ben Guppy descended the steps from our front door and made his way down to the driveway where his wife had been impatiently awaiting his return with Mr Axley from number twenty-eight. With every member of the party being hard of hearing, the hushed conversation was audible from fifty feet away. Pat Guppy, despairing at the state of the interior decoration of her home, as the Anaglypta had not received a coat of paint for more than a decade and the carpet, which had lived at the property longer than they had, was beginning to fall away in pieces, demanded her husband's reassurance that we could be forced to pay up, and do it quickly.

'We've got the Wittingworths coming next month,' she reminded him, 'and they've just re-carpeted their hall. We'll not hear the end of it if we don't make an effort.'

'We can't go wrong,' the old man said, 'Tom will back us up.'

There was silence from Tom Axley, but the progress of the conversation from that point suggested that he had not contradicted Ben Guppy's statement.

'And if they still refuse?' the old woman asked. 'What then? Do we wait to get this sorted out before we bring up the damp in the sitting room? That will cost a few thousand.'

'I'll sort it out!'

Tom Axley began making his excuses and attempted a hasty departure.

'You see what I have to put up with?' Ben Guppy asked his retreating ally. 'She's like this every day, all day.'

Tom Axley stood silent.

'What *you* have to put up with?' the old woman asked. 'Oh Tom, you've no idea what I suffer at this man's hands.'

'I'll sort it out!' Ben Guppy repeated.

'Like you sorted out the ceiling in the spare room? Like you did with the new light we were getting before Christmas? That was a sure thing wasn't it?'

'For God's sake woman,' Ben Guppy shouted, 'I'll take care of it so shut your mouth and leave me alone!'

'I told you, you've gone soft,' she stepped backwards as her husband moved towards her, 'you'll bugger this up just like you do everything else.'

'If you didn't keep on!' He took another step forwards and raised his fist towards the old woman's face. 'I've got it all worked out, I know what I'm doing.'

'You're a liar, you've been a liar since the day I married you,' the old woman said, 'you'll always be a liar, and a fool!'

'Come on now you two,' Tom Axley intervened, 'don't forget, it's them that's the enemy.'

With that, tempers were calmed. Tom Axley was instructed to put together a formal letter confirming his presence at the appearance of the ceiling puddles, the soaking of the curtains, and the shrinking of the carpet. Ben Guppy accepted his assignment, which was to pick up books of carpet samples so that a pattern could be chosen. And Pat Guppy, referring to the tremors in her knees, informed those present that she intended to go inside and call her doctor so that her medical health, and our negative impact upon it, would be documented for future reference.

Still to this day, I have no idea what made the Guppys believe that they had a chance of extracting large amounts of money from our bank account. True, the old woman's attempts at blackmail had proved to be relatively successful amongst the town's more well-known residents, who were so precious about their public image that a few hundred pounds every now and then probably seemed a reasonable price to pay for continued silence. In our case, however, there had been no lawless or adulterous act with which to construct a bargaining tool, and neither one of us had lost any sleep over the old pair's systematic destruction of our reputation. We had not faltered in our resolution never to give an inch, and yet they continued to attempt to take several miles. The Guppys were spurred on by the creation of so many notes, fuelled by their own activity and in need of none from us to increase their vigour and determination. Our continued silence was taken as a sign of imminent defeat and so, with each day that passed, the old pair's mood became more and more celebratory.

'I guarantee,' the old man said, when he and his wife passed Roy on the driveway as they made their way to their parked car, 'we'll be putting a deposit down on that carpet this weekend.' The old pair laughed out loud and headed for the street. Roy laughed inwardly and headed for home.

The weekend arrived so, with a spring in his step and a smile on his face, Ben Guppy made that all too familiar journey to the top of the stone steps outside our home and rapped his hand against the wooden door with great enthusiasm. When no answer came he lifted the letterbox and let it go with a snap. When this failed to acquire our attention he resorted to using the doorbell, three times.

'I know you're in there,' he called out through the letterbox. This was true. He had observed our return from a shopping trip, had listened to our footsteps as we ascended to the first floor, had awaited the sound of the key entering the lock and the subsequent closing of the front door. He had given us precisely two minutes to take off our coats and shoes, and to switch on the lights inside our home. Then, in a flurry of excitement, with his wife rushing out with him part of the way before feeling a few small drops of light rain and being forced to retreat indoors, he had set out to complete his mission. 'I say, I know you're in there!' he repeated.

'What's happening?' Pat Guppy called out from the old couple's doorway, frustrated by her inability to witness their moment of triumph by the sudden change in weather.

'There's no answer,' the old man said.

'What do you mean?'

'I mean they won't open the door.'

'Oh,' Pat Guppy replied, 'how rude!'

The old man began making his way back down onto the drive, holding the metal handrail as he descended, appearing to have had every last puff of wind taken out of his sails by our unwillingness to appear. His wife, somewhat vexed by her husband's lack of perseverance, called out to him to try harder.

'Get up there and do it yourself why don't you,' Ben Guppy said as he reached ground level, 'if you think you can do any better.'

As the old man rejoined his wife at the entrance to their home an argument broke out which, following the closure of their front door, continued within the flat below for the next two and a half hours. There were numerous accusations made by Pat Guppy, and an equivalent number of threats made by her husband. There was shouting, screaming, claims of an impending heart failure, the sound of kitchen equipment being hurled against a wall, much slamming of internal doors, and then a lengthy sobbing and wailing session which finished off the evening's dramatic entertainment.

The following day was a Wednesday. The third Wednesday in April to be precise. At half past eleven in the morning, with the purpose of heading off to a business appointment, Roy left our home and made his way to our car, which was parked on the driveway nearby. Unusually slow off the mark, Ben Guppy, upon hearing the sound of our car's engine start up, dashed out of his flat, propelled himself along the drive, waving his arms above his head and calling out for Roy to wait for him, and then, when he was alongside the passenger side of the car, which had by that time begun to crawl forward, he grabbed hold of the door handle and yanked away at it for all he was worth, shouting 'there's water pouring through the ceiling.' As the car reached the driveway's exit, and the old man stood a very good chance of being crushed between the passenger door and the solid stone gatepost nearby, Roy brought the car to a halt. He did so not out of some concern for the old man's safety, but rather out of concern for his own. Having contemplated the penalty for running down, or squashing between two hard surfaces, your elderly neighbour, Roy had concluded that he valued his freedom too much not to put his foot on the brake peddle.

As the car came to a standstill, Ben Guppy released his hold on the door's handle and shimmied between the car and the gatepost in order to make his way out onto the street. As he did so, he placed both hands upon the car's surface, maintaining contact as he slithered towards the bonnet and then continued around until he reached the driver side. He took hold of the door handle as he came parallel with Roy, tugging on it violently with one hand and, whilst tossing his head back and yelping, waved the other in the air in the fashion of an antiquated cowboy riding the bucking bronco. When he was finished waving he began pounding his fist against the side of the car, turning purple as he yanked and thumped, thumped and yanked. Then, having been unsuccessful in his attempt to gain access to the front of the vehicle, Ben Guppy leapt sideways, positioning himself alongside the rear passenger door, and pulled hard at the handle before beginning a sprint around the rear. The old man was fast, but not fast enough. Roy put his foot on the accelerator and, as he watched old Guppy dart from one side of his rear view mirror to the other, pulled the car forward.

'No,' the old man screamed, 'get back here!'

As Roy turned the car into the empty road and began to gain speed, Ben Guppy gave chase, managing to keep up for the first ten to fifteen feet before running out of steam and having to temporarily concede defeat. He stood in the centre of the road, bent forward with his hands resting on his knees, shaking his head and coughing. Then, in one last show of strength, raised his head, thrust both arms above his head, and screamed. He crouched, as if under starter's orders, and then lunged forward, breaking into a sprint for twenty feet before falling to his knees and rolling onto his side.

'Water,' he called out, 'through the ceiling.'

Mrs Palmer, who in truth could hardly tolerate the old man but considered it un-British not to pick up a neighbour who'd flung himself into the road, rushed out to ask if she could be of assistance. Informed by Ben Guppy that something had been pulled, she called for her husband who in turn called for Pat Guppy, who proceeded to kick the old man until he got up.

It is a sad fact of life that old people are generally considered to be harmless regardless of their conduct. The murderer, rapist, stalker or thief is granted a social pardon the moment he receives his senior citizen's bus pass. A young man will be judged on his own merits, but as he grows older and acquires wrinkles and white hair, or loses the latter almost entirely, an invisible halo forms above his head that assures him an unfair trial, decidedly in his favour, regardless of whatever crime he may commit. 'He's just an old man' is the response heard most often to any report of bad behaviour concerning a male of advancing years. Perhaps he did beat women when he was forty, but by the time he reaches sixty-five all that is forgotten and, for some unknown, is doubted to have ever taken place. Old people can do no great harm according to the vast majority of young and old alike, and this is a view which is shared by members of the police force, who should really know better. Unfortunately, we were unaware of this fact until a decision was made to call them in.

We were visited by PC Tony Hill on the Friday of the following week. In the days before that visit, possibly bolstered by his show of manly aggression and Roy's unwillingness to yield to any desire to punch the old fool regardless of how much he may have deserved it, Ben Guppy goaded both of us relentlessly. Pat Guppy joined in on several occasions, and Roy returned home from work each evening to the sound of the old woman shouting at him about her old age and our inconsiderate unwillingness to fund the purchase of their new carpet. She hurled abuse and accusations, and when that tactic appeared to yield no fruit began pleading to our conscience.

'He's an old man,' she protested, every time she caught sight of one of us, 'he's not long for this world.' Regarding the latter point, I had begun to hope that she was correct.

'He had to go for another CAT scan this evening,' she said to Roy, as he stepped out to pick up a newspaper, 'and his condition is serious. Don't you feel ashamed of what you're putting us through?'

But as I was saying, we were visited by PC Tony Hill on the Friday. I don't know what we had been expecting but it differed somewhat from what unfolded. Perhaps our lack of contact with those who commit crime or those who solve it up until that point had left us inadequately prepared for the news we received that day. We had, until then, harboured the childish belief that bad people are punished and good ones are protected. Of course that's all poppycock. PC Hill explained that there was little to be done. He went on to say that walking into a stranger's home without being invited whilst being in possession of a front door key was not a criminal offence. No law could prevent a man from chasing another man's car and, although it was frowned upon, there was no legal restriction placed upon the attempted opening of car doors, unless by force, when no criminal activity ensued after that point. Even if all of these things had been forbidden by law, he explained, our word alone would not have been enough to see the old man charged, so the legal status of each offence was beside the point. Of course the Guppys knew all of this. Their behaviour was calculated to be just bad enough to cause the maximum amount of distress whilst still remaining outside the boundaries of criminal law. He did, however, offer to have a word with them, despite the fact that he didn't believe a couple of old people could pose any real threat, in the hope that the mere sight of a uniform would make them see sense. And whilst we held out little hope that any amount of talking could reawaken something within the old pair which had long since withered and died, if indeed it had ever existed to begin with, the suggestion was welcomed by us, as was PC Hill's willingness to to let us know how things had gone after the fact.

Ben Guppy answered the door when the bell rang. According to PC Hill, when he telephoned shortly afterwards to report on the outcome of his endeavours, the old man was not visibly phased by the appearance of a policeman on his doorstep, and neither was his wife when she presented herself in the doorway. Perhaps this was the result of having received numerous not too dissimilar visits over the years. Who knows. What was certain was that they were prepared for a visit which up until a few days earlier we had not even considered requesting. Pat Guppy wasted no time in drawing the young man's attention to her friends in high places, including those within the local police force who occupied a far superior rank to that of the policeman before her, and she pointed out that she was well respected by local councillors and a friend to numerous members of parliament. Each point of concern raised by the young policeman was ignored by Pat Guppy in favour of a lengthy recollection of some important luncheon or dinner party attended by the Deputy Mayor and the local press. She reminded him that she had been featured in the local newspaper no less than three times during the previous twelve years, and that she had on more than one occasion been in the same building as Her Majesty the Queen.

Although far from being dissuaded when it came to continuing along their previous course, following PC Hill's visit the Guppys appeared to act with considerably less conviction. Having surmounted that preliminary hurdle with little effort, they seemed, nonetheless, to have suffered some anxiety as a result of receiving a visit from a local boy in blue. His defeat at their hands had reinforced their pre-existing belief that they were above the law, but he'd had the audacity to park his striped vehicle near to their front door, and the inconvenience of having to explain that away had caused them a little vexation. The news had spread like wild fire, and by the following Monday morning even the postman was asking after the fiasco on the drive, reports of which had by then evolved to include a whole squad of cars, numerous flashing lights, and a grapple on the street which had resulted in the arrest of Ben Guppy as he struggled to break free whilst wearing only his pyjamas and carpet slippers.

'I was not arrested,' Ben Guppy insisted, as he took hold of a small bundle of mail and gave the postman a sour look, 'that nice policeman was calling to check we were still alive, following threats against us by Mr Leah upstairs.' He gestured towards the first floor of the building and continued, 'we're having to have round the clock protection now.'

The postman was silent.

'I tell you it's true,' the old man protested, 'we're the victims in all this. Just you go and ask the neighbours, they'll tell you all about it.'

Silence.

'Well,' the old man said, 'I can see you're going to take their side. Get off, go on, sod off,' he concluded, before swinging his fists about and threatening to kick the postman's arse if he came back again.

Pat Guppy, still convinced that having us cast out of polite society was the best way to bring us in line, proceeded to play the victim to anyone who would listen, entertaining them with tales of our late night loiterings on the drive, which were apparently intended to strike fear into the old woman's heart and bring about her untimely death, and threats to the old man's person as, risking life and limb, he made the terrifying journey from the old couple's front door to their garage. Pleas for help, accompanied by much wailing and gnashing of the teeth, were made to neighbours to inspire a feeling of sympathy amongst all who dwelled nearby. And when the neighbours were considered to be well enough informed, the Guppys cast their net wide and wailed and gnashed at any stranger who passed by in the street or happened to stand behind them in a queue at the supermarket.

Their immense effort was wasted, however, as we continued to ignore their demands for money and their carpet and curtains remained unchanged. Frustrated by their lack of progress, the old pair appeared to flounder for a few days, turning on each other when no other avenue presented itself as a means of letting off copious amounts of steam. Then a change took place. Ben Guppy, who had focused almost all of his attention on Roy for the previous few months, began to single me out for some of his special treatment. He had continued to observe and monitor our movements for some time, so that in itself was not unusual, but the purpose of this observation evolved into something considerably more sinister as May gave way to June and the warmer weather arrived. Concealed from unwanted prying eyes, behind the then flourishing climbing plants which had regained their foliage following the winter freeze, whilst remaining in plain sight to anyone unfortunate enough to observe him from our kitchen or study window, the old man stood, with one hand thrust deep inside his front trouser pocket, playing pocket billiards for five to ten minutes at a time. Then, operating under the illusion that his performance had caused considerable offence, he'd strut up and down the drive proudly forty or so times, before heading off to the rear of the building and settling back in behind his trellis with his camera, taking the odd break throughout the day when his wife joined him with tea and a newspaper. If the weather turned, and the old pair were forced indoors, they took to banging on the ceiling below my feet, or hammering on the pipes in their kitchen and, judging by the whoops and jeers that were emitted from the rooms below, they enjoyed themselves immensely whilst doing so. As Roy arrived home from work, however, the noise would stop, and after two weeks of regular repeat performances, Pat Guppy awaited his return beneath the stone steps that led to our flat, and picked her moment as he began to unload bags of shopping from the boot of our car.

'You must worry about your wife being here alone when you're away on business,' she began, 'but if you'd be a bit more neighbourly I could make sure that Ben never bothers her. Good neighbours look after each other.'

She explained that her husband had a very bad temper indeed, and was prone to violent, and sometimes sexual, outbursts at the drop of a hat. She described his inability to think rationally at times, and said she was worried that a person could get caught up in the middle of one of his rages quite easily and very unexpectedly. She expressed her heartfelt desire to become friends with us, and to see that no harm came to me in particular, and then she presented her terms.

'Settle your accounts,' she said, smiling.

'In your dreams,' Roy replied.

'It's either that or suffer the consequences. You can't go damaging...'

'We didn't damage your property, you interfering old crone. You want your pigsty decorated? Pay for it yourself. Do you think I was born yesterday? If you ever...' he paused, moved a step closer, and lowered his voice, 'try something like this again. I'll kill you. Do you hear me?'

The stunned expression on Pat Guppy's face confirmed that she had heard Roy's words. And, at that point in time at least, she had believed them. She scurried off towards the safety of her home as fast as her gammy knees would carry her, hobbled up the step outside her front door, turned to ascertain Roy's whereabouts, fearful that he had rushed after her to do the job straight away, and then disappeared inside. The sound of the door slamming hard was followed by that of the old woman calling out to her husband. 'He's going to kill me! Ben, he said he's going to kill me! My pills, give me my pills!'

CHAPTER THREE

POISON. I know nothing about the subject, but it appears to be a very useful thing to have around if you are intending to kill a person and have regular access to their meals. But I still wasn't that far along, so even if the thought had crossed my mind, and I can't say categorically that it never did, I most certainly wouldn't have acted on it. Besides, I would have found it next to impossible to get my hands on whatever the Guppys thought passed for food. I don't know what they ate each day, but judging by the cooking smells which rose up from the Guppys' flat and made their way into ours, and at times made me feel so sick to my stomach that it was necessary for me to open a window and stick my head out of it, their food intake was probably capable of ending a human life without the addition of any toxic chemical.

Poison was on the mind of Ben Guppy though. But not the kind that does away with humans. No. He was concerned with the kind that does away with your neighbour's garden plants. I've no idea when it started, but I looked out of the window one morning that May to see the old man take a handful of powder from his trouser pocket and throw it onto our garden border alongside the driveway. It explained a lot. Our little garden was small and far from perfect, but it was much loved and we'd gone to great expense to empty the flower bed of weeds and replant it with small flowering shrubs and climbers just a month earlier. We had been very confused as to why so few of the plants had survived more than a week or so, and our confusion had increased further still when, after replacing the dead plants with healthy new specimens, all additions to our garden had suffered the same fate as their predecessors just days after planting.

As the old man was a creature of habit, I returned to the window at the same time the following morning, and the one after that, and each day after that for the remainder of the week. The old man's routine followed the same pattern more or less each time. He left his flat at about ten o'clock in the morning and walked along the driveway to his garage at the rear of the property. He opened one of the garage doors and took a handful of the unidentified powder from a bag just by the entrance. Then, after pausing to make sure that he hadn't been observed, he would disappear behind the leafy trellis for a moment before making his way along the driveway towards our garden border. As he reached the spot just opposite his own front door, which was shielded from potential witnesses in the nearby street by a dense wall of ivy, he would look to his wife, who had been awaiting his arrival and monitoring traffic, for a sign that the coast was clear, and then hurl a handful of the toxic mixture onto the soil. Halting momentarily to ascertain the effectiveness of his tossing, he would walk the rest of the driveway, travelling beyond its exit and around the corner until he was out of sight. He would pause for a moment and then return along the drive in the direction of his own front door and, upon receiving a congratulatory pat on the back from his foreman, or a reprimand for having missed a bit, would return indoors.

I might never have noticed what the old man was doing the first time I caught him, however, had it not been for the behaviour of his wife only a day or so before. The postman had attempted to deliver a parcel to us, and as I reached the door, after taking some time to get out of bed and find a suitable robe, I heard the old woman call out that he shouldn't bother ringing again as we were not home. As I looked out of the window to the right of the front door, only to see the postman disappearing behind the gatepost as he exited the drive and went on his merry way, I watched in disbelief as Pat Guppy emptied the contents of a small plastic bag onto our garden, shaking it repeatedly to make sure that every last scrap of paper had fallen to the ground. There was always more than the customary share of rubbish scattered around our shrubbery, but we had assumed up until that morning that strong winds, which were so common with us being right on the coast, had blown the various pieces of paper and bits of plastic wrapping onto our property from the street. With the suspicion that she might have been doing this regularly in mind, I kept a close eye on our garden for the following few days. And sure enough, each morning she would toss a bit of paper here, a sandwich wrapper there, or a bag of vegetable peelings pretty much everywhere. If I was incredibly lucky, and I thank the heavens that I was rarely blessed with such good fortune, the old woman would have no scraps from indoors to toss and would be forced to recover some from her own garden or the nearby pavement before depositing them amongst our greenery. As she leaned forward to acquire fresh supplies, taking some considerable time to bend down far enough to accomplish her task, and twice as long to straighten up afterwards, I was treated to a full-on wide-screen view of her backside. It just so happened, on that one particular day in May, that her bending, and my wincing, was followed by the old man adding his own special concoction to the soil beneath our lilac tree.

Much to my amazement, and that is saying something because little the old pair did brought about so much as a raised eyebrow by that time, only a few days after witnessing the powder-tossing for the first time, I was treated to a display which for days afterwards I considered might have been an hallucination as it seemed so utterly bizarre. On the day in question, after unloading his pocket of powder, the old man seemed confused and wandered back and forth as if in a daze. He headed towards his own front door and then, upon appearing to change his mind regarding his planned destination, walked a few steps towards our garden. He walked a few paces back towards his front door, then a few more towards our steps, and then finally headed off towards his garden at the rear of the drive. Upon reaching his garden, he mounted the rickety wooden bench within it and, with arms waving about above his head and a much expanded version of that usual crooked grin upon his face, he began to howl like a dog.

'Howooo,' went the old man. 'Grrr, how, how, howoooooo!'

I can't say that this display was intended for my benefit. The fact that Ben Guppy was far from insane at the time leads me to believe now that his constant efforts to be seen as being one bun short of a bun-ring were intended to provide him with a defence, that of a deteriorating mental state due to old age, in the event that he was caught committing a crime or alleged to have committed one. I never saw him howl again, but over the following months I did sometimes see him barking, or occasionally calling out to some invisible assailant to get off and leave him alone.

But back to the poisoning. It, like so many of the things the Guppys did, was not considered, by the local boys in blue, to be an offence worth pursuing. They did not, apparently, have the man power or financial resources to go about the place collecting soil samples to solve the riddle of the shrivelled Saxifrage. They suggested that, if we really objected so strongly to our growables being assassinated, we should find a good solicitor, install closed circuit television, catch the old pair in the act, and provide unquestionable evidence with which to construct a civil case. Either that, or dig up every living thing and leave the old pair nothing to kill off.

'What's a few plants in the greater scheme of things?' one policewoman asked.

'An outlay of about £200 and a lot of backbreaking digging,' Roy replied. His comment sprouted wings and flew over the young officer's head at speed.

'Not worth losing sleep over,' she went on.' Come back if it's you they're trying to poison.' All uniforms present sniggered.

A lengthy search for the right solicitor resulted in one discussion with a Mrs Fairbanks, of Fairbanks, Dewey and Fisk. That one discussion resulted in another, this time with an electrician by the name of Gus Harper, which in turn resulted in the ordering of one alarm system, one CCTV system, and the hiring of a very, very long ladder.

The fitting of the alarm, one sunny morning in June, brought both the old man and his wife out onto the driveway in a flurry of vexed excitement to see what was happening. They appeared to find its installation annoying, confusing, and strangely fascinating at the same time. The old man followed Theo, Gus Harper's young apprentice, about the place and stood monitoring his comings and goings as he went to fetch more tools from the small white van that was parked nearby. He carried with him the usual pen and paper with which to jot down activities of note and, dangling upon a chord which hung from his boney wrist, the old man's trusty Polaroid swung in the summer breeze, loaded and ready to shoot anyone who looked sideways at its master. The old woman rushed indoors to change her clothes before emerging in the blackest of black short-sleeved knitted tops, and then trundled off to fetch a few similarly sour-faced compadres to observe the electrician and his mate at work. Upon her return she positioned herself at the edge of the drive, with feet spread apart and arms folded, and ordered her troupe to attention.

'You see,' she said, 'how they cause disruption without giving a thought to my knees.'

There were sighs and tuts from the assembled crowd.

The testing of the alarm, and the shrill pulse that emanated from the plastic casing just above our front door, had the old couple and their entourage rushing this way and that before congregating at the foot of our steps. Pat Guppy clapped her ears to the sides of her head and grimaced. Her drones followed suit.

'I must protest,' she said. 'This has gone on long enough!'

Rushing to the foot of the ladder, which was propped up against the wall alongside our front door with Gus Harper at the top of it, the old woman took hold of both sides and shook it hard.

'Come down at once, do you hear. Stop that right now!'

'Bugger off,' came Gus Harper's reply.

The assembled cronies gasped and took one step back. Ben Guppy raised his camera and attempted to capture the verbal assault on film.

'Come away,' the old man cautioned. 'We don't know what these people are capable of.' There were more gasps from the stunned crowd.

The installation of the CCTV cameras, one week later, was an even more dramatic event. The moment Gus arrived the old couple took their positions on dilapidated deckchairs at the rear of the drive. They were very well prepared, with a flask of tea, a plate of sandwiches, and a selection of newspapers and magazines, but the reading matter wasn't taken along to provide a diversion when the entertainment became tiresome. No, they were there to provide a disguise behind which to observe the proceedings without appearing too obvious. Raised up to conceal the occupants of the brightly coloured outdoor seating, they twitched at every sound and were cast aside in an instant the moment Gus Harper attempted to extend his ladder to its optimum length. The old man shot out of his seat and rushed to his garage. He got into his car and, after much juddering about as he reversed the vehicle out of the flimsy wood-fronted structure, almost knocking his wife onto her backside as she attempted to drag her seat and herself off the drive, drove it towards Gus and his extended ladder. The car came to a stop. The old man sat, waiting expectantly, as Gus and his apprentice were forced to move the large and cumbersome apparatus off the drive to allow him to pass by. The fetching of the car had obviously been designed to cause the maximum amount of disruption, for no sooner had the ladder been repositioned against the wall, with much effort on the part of Gus and his young helper, than the old man was driving back up along the driveway and insisting that it be moved again. He did this repeatedly until Gus, having had more than enough of him, refused to move one more time.

And once the cameras were in position the question and answer section of the programme began.

'Will these cameras film me in my garden?' the old man asked, as Gus took up a mug of tea to quench his thirst after a hot morning's work.

'Do they swivel?' he went on. 'Can they see inside the building?'

Gus continued drinking.

'Did they...' the old man turned and pointed in my direction, as I descended the stone steps to the side of the building and headed for our garden. 'Did they get planning permission for this surveillance equipment?'

Gus remained silent.

'I won't stand for it,' Ben Guppy went on. 'There will be words about this at the local council.'

Believing that the prospect of being caught on film doing something morally or legally questionable would be enough of a deterrent to force the old pair to reconsider their behaviour towards us, we assumed, quite prematurely as it turned out, that we were about to see an end to the spying, following, poisoning, photographing, and public genitalia fondling which had been par for the course during the preceding ten months. We found the Guppys' visible distress at the appearance of those cameras, their frustration when Gus refused to remove them, and their apparent inability to conceal both from us, to be highly amusing. And in the days that followed we laughed at the sight of the pair of them, rushing around the street, knocking on the doors of potential allies to drum up support for their campaign to have the intrusive surveillance equipment removed. Pat Guppy, customarily outfitted in black and with the usual clipboard in hand, went about the place shaking hands and kissing babies, and pointing out the decreased flexibility in her left leg, while her husband, turning purple on cue to demonstrate the severe deterioration within his cranium since our arrival, concentrated his attention on the local postal workers who, he assured his wife, would be aptly placed to spread the word.

We did, of course, receive the inevitable call from the local planning officer a little while later. With camera and measuring tape in hand he surveyed, photographed, and noted down the particulars of the arrangement of small globular cameras which, from high off the ground, monitored his steady progress. A short conversation a little while later revealed that, in accordance with his findings, one of the cameras needed to be moved a couple of feet to the right. We shook hands, promising to see that the necessary alteration was made, and parted company.

'You see,' Pat Guppy said to Roy, as he ignored her on the way to our car. 'You'll know better than to play games with us in future.' Then, noticing Bob Brandt from number fourteen crossing the street in the direction of the local post box, she waved her hand in the air and called out to him. 'Did you hear the news Bob? The cameras are coming down!'

A couple of weeks passed in relative peace following the installation of the cameras. The old pair were quite phased by the cameras, but whilst they were furious about their existence, they appeared to be rather curious as to their workings. The old man paced back and forth, watching the lights on the sensors flashing as his movement was detected. He walked around the driveway trying to determine the area covered by each camera, and hid behind his trellis or our garden wall before jumping out to see how quickly each one became aware of his presence. With these things to occupy his time, he appeared too busy to bother following us about, and we went about our daily lives without being bothered by him or his wife. Of course the novelty wore off. And as soon as he had a basic understanding of what he was dealing with, and had determined that there wasn't a way to avoid being filmed when out on the driveway, he began conjuring up new ways to make his presence felt without having to venture into the camera's view, believing that such measures would be temporary as the cameras were, according to his wife who had 'someone inside' at the planning department, coming down at any moment.

Of course, the cameras' filming capabilities were limited to the property itself, and did not include the nearby streets, and the old man soon found that you could toss a pocketful of powder just as easily from behind a waist high garden wall as you could from a driveway. He also discovered that powder wasn't the only thing worth throwing from that vantage point. In the few weeks that followed the planning officer's final inspection of the adjusted camera and subsequent confirmation that all three could stay, and possibly fuelled by his anger when he was made aware of this outcome, the old man deposited numerous things over the wall, including a recycling bin, various carrier bags, several newspapers, a half-eaten porkpie, the odd bundle of twigs, and a shopping basket. Not long after that, when the depositing of those items had proved most unrewarding because the response he had expected had not been forthcoming, the old man took to climbing onto our garden, crushing anything that happened to be underfoot, to retrieve whatever had been thrown immediately following its landing. And during each of these deposits and subsequent removals, his elderly wife, with Polaroid in hand, stood nearby awaiting the call to snap the scene, should we appear and threaten to throttle him.

An attempt, on Roy's part, to enlist the assistance of the local community police officer brought with it the suggestion that we should stay indoors as much as possible, as placing yourself in the vicinity of someone who obviously means you harm makes you at least half responsible after the fact if you happen to be beaten to death.

'They'll soon get tired of trying to poison your garden,' the WPC reassured us, 'when every last one of your plants is dead.'

Perhaps in the belief that none of his activities had been witnessed, and possibly as a result of increased back pain from lifting all of those bins and boxes on and off our garden for the previous four weeks, the old man seemed to lose interest in throwing anything over the wall as we reached the middle of July. It was at that point that the powder disappeared and the garden tools made their first appearance. While Ben Guppy went to fetch a garden fork and a small spade from his garage, Pat Guppy inspected what was left of the plants in our garden, pushing at them with the toe of her sandals and cursing them for being so resilient before standing on their heads. Upon returning to his wife with the necessary implements, the old man handed her the small spade, and she stepped back politely to allow him space to manoeuvre as he drove the fork into our garden soil and began moving it back and forth, left and right, to loosen the roots of his chosen plant. As he raised his fork from the ground and moved on to the next spot of vegetation, the old woman moved in with her spade and raised the poor plant out of the ground before flinging it against the garden wall. She stopped every now and then to pull the leaves off any shrub that she considered too large for them to remove entirely, and her husband carried on along the length of the garden until every last plant was free from the soil and lying with roots exposed.

You'd think, wouldn't you, that even if spying on your neighbours and following them about, or letting yourself into their home was considered outside the boundaries of the criminal justice system, the digging up of their garden would warrant a certain amount of action on the part of the boys in blue. Alas no.

'Mr and Mrs Guppy could quite comfortably claim that they were attempting to weed your garden,' the community officer explained, when Roy telephoned the local police station for guidance. 'To help you out. They are just an old couple after all. The plants can be replaced, so there's been no permanent damage done.'

Ironically, the old couple were more visibly upset by our unwillingness to react to their actions than we were by the fact that they had acted in the first place. I imagine that it had taken some effort to entirely extract our largest lavender bush from the dry hard soil, and they had most likely suffered some muscle pain in the process. They had returned indoors with sweaty brows and dirty footwear, and their aged spade, structurally compromised by too many days and nights exposed to the elements, had snapped under the pressure of the old woman's body weight during the removal of the last withered Fuchsia bush. Having given up an entire afternoon to this activity, and having received no reward for their efforts, the old pair spent the remainder of the evening shouting at each other and slamming doors repeatedly until, at about two o'clock in the morning, the building fell silent.

The Guppys were spending a lot of time arguing by that point. But their shouting and door slamming rarely took place whilst our other neighbours within the building were at home. By the end of July you could pretty much guarantee that, upon the departure of those who worked for a living, the old couple would begin to scream at each other at the tops of their voices, and that this rowdy dialogue would make its way out onto the drive and into their garden at the rear before elevenses. The old woman's shrill declarations that she couldn't go on for much longer with discoloured wall coverings and threadbare carpeting, which emanated from behind the pale pinks and soft oranges of scented climbing plants, were usually met by the old man's violent reassurances, usually bellowed from the top of a ladder while he tried to adjust the focus of his binoculars, that he would sort us out by the end of the day. He was rarely willing to go any further and describe just how he proposed doing this, as his statement of intent was considered, by him at least, to be all the response that was necessary. And if Pat Guppy pushed him for details she would be summarily told to 'shut it.'

I learned rather a lot from those heated dialogues, and from them formed a picture of the Guppys and their inner workings which made it possible to prepare for and combat many of their ill thought out attempts to pry money loose from our bank account over the following months before they were even able to get their plans off the ground, and in the passage of time to formulate possible ways to do away with them once and for all if the need ever arose. I became quite familiar with their thought processes, and despite feeling quite unclean as a result of being so exposed to the not so private life of the old pair, valued those outbursts for the information they imparted.

Whilst I don't believe that the old couple's behaviour towards us had originally been motivated by any personal dislike, and had focused entirely upon the acquisition of wealth, it had, over the previous months, become very personal indeed. Financial gain was still very present in their minds when any plan concerning us was being hatched, but their hatred of us had taken its place as their primary motivation. We had dared to refuse them rights which they considered to be an unquestionable entitlement of old age and superior breeding, and had on more than one occasion left them looking utterly foolish. The old woman had been quite competent at wielding the threat of action from friends in high places to keep those around her in their place, compliant, and reliant upon her good opinion of them. But we had called her bluff and she had been exposed as lacking. No thunderbolt had pierced the sky and landed on our heads when we denied them access to our home and bank account and, as far as those in the neighbouring properties were concerned at least, we appeared to show no fear at the possibility that this could befall us at any moment.

Deeply concerned when it came to being filmed doing something questionable, the old pair gave no thought whatsoever to being heard discussing the same activity. Careful to remain out of the cameras' field of view, as they contemplated the most prudent course of action at that point, they took no precautions to make sure they were not overheard. And so, as I sat at the top of the steps just outside our front door, painting the weathered frame, the old couple stood only five feet away, out of sight, discussing their chances of getting one or both of us arrested.

'Well, you can hardly say he tried to run you down in his car now can you?' the old woman said. 'They would have those tapes from that damned machine of theirs to prove he didn't, and you'd be left with egg on your face.'

The old man agreed.

'And likewise, I can't go saying he assaulted me now either.'

'That's not strictly true,' the old man interjected. 'You could say he came to the front door and hit you. The cameras don't film there, I checked.'

'I'd need bruises.'

'I'll give you some.'

'Oh no you won't!'

'Come now my dear,' the old man said. 'It will hurt me more to give them than it will you to receive them. And I promise to avoid your glasses.'

The old woman wasn't convinced.

The Guppys had already begun crying to the neighbours that it was our intention to set about them one dark night, and had insisted that they feared for their lives. Pat Guppy informed Roy one evening, as he took out bags of rubbish for collection the following day, that everyone in the street was talking about us, and that several neighbours were so concerned that they had offered the old woman a bed for the night, to remove the possibility that she would be beaten to death while she slept. In the meantime, Ben Guppy was insisting, to anyone who would listen, that we were intending to force the old pair out of their happy home of numerous years in order to move my family in, and that my relatives were, according to reliable sources, a bunch of bruisers.

So, as the summer turned to autumn, this was where we found ourselves; living above a couple of malicious old fools who were determined to have us incarcerated for grievous bodily harm. Everywhere we turned there were fingers being pointed, accusations flying this way and that, and little huddles of elderly people standing on street corners sharing the latest hot gossip they had gleaned about us without ever having uttered a word in our direction. As the weeks passed and the accusations multiplied, however, the notion of that imminent brutal assault, which had sprung forth from the malevolent minds of the old couple, began to take root in my own.

CHAPTER FOUR

A MEDIUM sized courgette. That was what greeted Roy as he made his way around to the side of our car one chilly morning during the first week in September. It had not been present on the drive as he descended the steps, but upon reaching the bottom it had been hurled from the doorway of the Guppys' flat, and had landed three feet or so away from him, losing a small section of it's deep green shiny surface upon impact, and had rolled another couple of feet before coming to a stop. The old man, face contorted and fists clenched, was standing outside his front door, mumbling to himself and turning a deep shade of purple. Having lost the ability to be surprised by the old pair, Roy calmly opened the rear door on the passenger side of our car, placed his briefcase on the back seat, and then made his way around to the driver side before climbing into his seat, closing his door, and pulling away from the building. He did not speak to the old man. He did not look at the old man beyond that initial glance to confirm the identity of the courgette tosser. But in his rear view mirror he could see Ben Guppy standing there by his door, shaking furiously and stamping his foot.

Whilst the chosen method of communication wasn't entirely expected, the attempt on Ben Guppy's part to make his presence felt that day was no great surprise. That solitary winter vegetable served as a response to a letter which had arrived on the Guppys' doormat that morning, from Mrs Fairbanks, of

Fairbanks, Dewey and Fisk. We were not concerned with the claims made to neighbours, or those which the old pair were just beginning to make to the Environmental Health Department, but we took the prospect of spending hours at a police station, regardless of the inevitable release due to the complete absence of evidence, very seriously indeed. After careful consideration, and some lengthy discussion regarding the cost of a civil law suit, we finally concluded that the time was right to enlist the help of a solicitor. Mrs Fairbanks spoke at length about hitting the old pair head on with all guns blazing. We gave her a brief description of the events which had taken place up to that point, and she voiced her determination to see that we didn't have to continue living in such unbearable conditions for much longer. She drafted a letter almost immediately, and by the end of business the following day sent it out by first class post. The screams from below us, on the day the courgette appeared, alerted us to the fact that the letter had arrived.

After rushing back and forth, and at one point running after the postman to show him the contents of the mail just received, Ben Guppy returned to the driveway still wearing his pyjamas, and proceeded to kick the only shrub brave enough to remain standing following their last assault. He hung around the bottom of our steps for some time, waiting for one of us to appear. And, after twenty minutes or so of waiting and shouting and turning from red to purple, and from purple to blue and then back to red, the old man stormed off down the drive towards his garage. He opened one of the large wooden doors and returned to that sizeable bag of off-white powder and, after throwing a plastic bowl of some sort around the driveway and being forced to rummage through his garden plants to locate it again, scooped up a large quantity of the mixture before heading back along the drive and emptying the entire contents onto our garden. Pat Guppy emerged at that point, half-dressed and complaining, as she'd been forced to cut her ablutions short, and tried to restrain the old man, reminding him that he was in plain sight of the cameras. She pulled at his dressing gown, yanking him towards their doorway, and snatched the container from his hand before hurling it over the garden wall.

'I will not calm down,' the old man protested. 'The bloody nerve of these two!'

'Come inside at least,' his wife suggested, drawing his attention to the flashing red light attached to the camera just twenty feet above their heads.

'I don't care!' The old man raised his fist above his head and drummed it at the four inch black plastic ball looking back at him.

'Bastards! Bastards!'

The old woman tightened her grip and yanked the old man towards their hallway.

'Bastaaaaaaaards!'

Then the courgette appeared, and Roy went off to work.

The postman, who had neglected to deliver one piece of mail and was therefore forced to return to the driveway as Ben Guppy was being removed from it, had been loitering near the gateway, waiting for the noise to subside. Prepared to flee at the first sign of movement, he set out towards the old couple's front door, silently placing one foot before the other whilst holding his postal sack close to his body to prevent it from rustling as he made his approach. This sight was not unusual. The old man's fascination with the post office and all of its workers was the subject of much discussion amongst those who lived locally and all who worked at the local depot. He regularly waited at the corner of the road when the postman was due to arrive, and took every opportunity to distract the young man whilst attempting to examine the mail intended for his neighbours, before following the poor chap down the road as he continued on his rounds. Every now and then, Ben Guppy would persuade some temporary postal replacement that he was eager to assist in the delivery of the mail, and would manage to pry a bundle of letters from the postman's hand under the pretence that he wished to see them delivered to their rightful owners. On such a day, the old man could be seen jumping up and down at the corner of the road, almost unable to contain his excitement, gleefully convinced that the papers clasped in his hot little hands would divulge some hidden secret that could be used later on for financial gain. But the unfortunate postal worker had brought him nothing but bad tidings that day and was a marked man.

'What is it this time?' the old man asked.

The Guppys' front door was flung open just as the young postman reached his destination.

'Do you think I've got nothing better to do with my time than read the shite you bring me?'

The postman stood silent.

'Shite! You come here with nothing but shite!'

The young man took two steps backwards.

'Shite!'

Four more steps.

'Here, take it back. I don't want your shite!'

As the old man stepped forward and thrust the crumpled envelope out as far as his reach would take it, the young postman

73

jumped three more steps backwards, attempting a partial turn as he did so. The old man, tossing the letter into the air as he pulled his robe around him, leapt off his doorstep and prepared to make chase. Pat Guppy, taking hold of her husband's sleeve and refusing to release her grip, called out to the postman to run for it, which he did without delay. Ben Guppy, pulling away from his wife in an attempt to release his sleeve from her grip and realising that his efforts were futile, extracted himself from his dressing gown and made off across the drive in a pair of pale blue cotton pyjamas, with his thin white comb-over losing its hold on his bald pate as he picked up speed, flapping back and forth in the breeze as the old man turned onto the street and darted along the road.

Following the old man's return, which took place five minutes after his exit and was heralded by the sound of Mrs Palmer calling out from the garden next door to ask if he needed a physician, the Guppys passed the remainder of the day screaming at each other, banging doors, thumping something against the ceiling beneath our bedroom, and walking up and down the drive insisting, whilst shouting directly at our bedroom window, that we should leave them alone and learn to have some respect for our elders and betters. The old man then concluded his show of outrage by throwing handfuls of soil onto the stone steps which led up to our home, and hurling pebbles at the CCTV cameras.

The day following the arrival of the letter, we received a telephone call from our solicitor. She informed Roy that the old couple had been in touch that morning, and that she was beginning to have some concerns about our case. After declaring their innocence and informing Mrs Fairbanks that we were quite determined to see them cast out into the street, penniless and destitute, Pat Guppy had gone on to say that she and her husband were perfectly willing to sit down and discuss the situation in a friendly manner, as they had for some time sincerely hoped that at some point in the not too distant future we would all get along famously. She expressed a desire to say 'hello neighbour' when she passed us on the drive in the morning, and to exchange Christmas cards and the like. She stressed her feelings of disbelief and horror following the arrival of the solicitor's letter the previous day, as they had, she assured Mrs Fairbanks, never had a cross word with any neighbour in the past. And our solicitor, despite being hired to represent our interests, had sought to calm the old woman's distress and had indicated to both Pat and Ben Guppy, as she had spoken to both at length, that she would persuade us against taking the matter to court. Mrs Fairbanks had managed to do something which the old couple had ceased being able to do for some months. She had left us speechless.

The courgette was followed by a lettuce one weeks later, and the arrival of a written response to Mrs Fairbanks' letter, which was forwarded on to us. We had assumed that there would be counter claims, accusations, and perhaps the threat of retaliatory legal action if we pursued the matter, and all of that was present so there were no surprises there. It was the nature of the accusations, however, which surprised us.

'Dear Mrs Fairbanks,' the letter began. 'We were surprised, neigh stunned, to receive your letter containing such heinous accusations regarding myself and my elderly and ailing wife. As I informed you during our telephone conversation, I am unwell myself. I have undergone several scans, due to the extreme anxiety caused by this situation, as I had a tumour ten years ago. My doctor thought it would be most prudent to scan my brain to check if it had come back. I must inform you that any action on your part will be met with equal force on ours, as we are in the process of commencing a legal case of our own. It is our intention to sue Mr and Mrs Leah for harassment, intimidation, invasion of privacy, libel, slander, and discrimination.'

'Firstly, Mr and Mrs Leah have installed electronic hearing equipment within our ceiling with the purpose of listening in on private conversations within our home. Secondly, Mr Leah has attempted on more than one occasion to influence the postman's good opinion of me and has blackened my name to the local postmaster. I have never attempted to manhandle the mail or its deliverer and am outraged at the suggestion that I would consider doing any such thing. Thirdly, Mr and Mrs Leah have been pouring water into our flat and have refused to pay for the damage. There are, at this time, in excess of nine outstanding claims which need to be seen to immediately. The carpet is soaked and this must be replaced as my wife has begun to suffer from extreme dampness. Fourthly, surveillance equipment has been installed by Mr and Mrs Leah for the sole purpose, as they admitted to the electrician who did the fitting, of catching my wife and myself in the act of doing something criminal. We demand that this be removed so that we can return to our usual mode of living. Lastly, Mr Leah has stolen my milk bottles and might also be responsible for the fishy smell coming from my electricity meter. I will keep you informed with regards to that last point. Yours Sincerely, Mr Benjamin Arnold Guppy Esq.'

Regarding electronic hearing equipment, there was some lengthy discussion amongst our neighbours in the days that followed Ben Guppy's letter, which the old pair had made publicly available, and several came to the conclusion that we must indeed have it. A couple stopped us on the drive to ask what we had heard, and were disappointed that there was no recording for sale to the public. James Floyd commented, when Roy asked him where this equipment was supposed to be situated, that the old man had indicated some area within the ventilation shafts between the Guppys' ceiling and our floor.

'There are no ventilation shafts,' Roy explained, to a man who knew this all too well already. 'So how can you give this nonsense the time of day?'

'Well,' Floyd responded. 'Why would they make this up?'

News of our listening devices spread like wild fire and, coupled with the existence of the closed circuit TV cameras, which Ben Guppy had assured everyone were capable of filming through solid brick walls, had Mrs Palmer from next door believing Roy's employment might even be within the secret service. Pat Guppy complained to Mr Axley from number twenty-eight that we filmed them when they prepared and ate their dinner, when they went to bed, and even when they took a bath. And people listened. And people believed.

In light of the nature of Ben Guppy's written response, we had assumed that Mrs Fairbanks would come to her senses and advise us as to the next step, with a clear head and with no misconceptions regarding the innocent and harmless nature of our elderly neighbours. Alas, the effects of conversing with either of the Guppys for longer than half an hour seemed to be irreversible, and despite the fact that the old man's reply in no way satisfied the demands contained within our solicitor's letter to him, Mrs Fairbanks still advocated a meeting with tea and biscuits, and advised that we should turn the other cheek. Her reasons for suggesting this were no longer motivated by her belief that the old pair were indeed innocent. Not in the slightest. She had, after careful consideration, come to the conclusion that the old man was mentally ill, and that we should therefore make allowances.

The lettuce was followed a few days later by a suede. It was thrown from the Guppy's doorway in the usual fashion and narrowly missed Roy's head before bouncing off the wall opposite and landing with a thump on the drive. The old man had cried out 'have that!' before the vegetable was jettisoned into space, and had followed it with a small turnip.

I am not sure what prevented Roy from throttling Ben Guppy that day. He was certainly angry enough to do it when he returned to our flat. But he had promised almost a year previously that he would never speak to the man again, and that he would most certainly never lay a finger on him. I had made no such promise of course. And whilst I don't believe that I had begun contemplating murder at that point, I am sure that the idea of a certain amount of physical injury was beginning to appear acceptable. Indeed, it was most likely starting to appear quite necessary.

Whilst the suede and turnip still lay on the driveway, a cauliflower joined them. Having been tossed unceremoniously at a painter and decorator who was visiting our flat, after the old man mistook him for Roy, it hit the tarmac hard and scattered body parts across the surface of the drive. The painter, like everyone else who visited our home, had been warned before arriving that he should expect a certain amount of odd activity from the old couple and, apart from giving the old man a rather violent two finger salute, continued about his business without batting an eyelid.

Pat Guppy stood beneath the steep flight of stone steps that led to our flat as Roy discussed the work we were planning with the painter. It was where she stood whenever anyone called at our door. If she was otherwise occupied, the old man would be sent out to stand in for her. And on those rare occasions when the old man did not reach that spot in time, or had failed to hear the contents of the conversation above due to being almost completely deaf in one ear, he would be instructed to rush after our caller in the hope of gleaning some small amount of information by means of a speedy interrogation alongside the front gatepost. A visit from a tradesman always resulted in an elevated level of annoyance downstairs, and there had been quite a few arguments during the previous few weeks concerning our ability to afford the work we were carrying out, and the old couple's right to some portion of the money we were spending on it. Exclamations concerning their unwillingness to stand by and watch us whittle away at the money pot they'd set their sights on, along with door slamming and saucepan hurling, had followed every tradesman's call. The painter's visit was no exception.

A note arrived an hour or so after the painter's departure. There was, according to the old man, more water inside the flat beneath us, and the wetness was apparently due to the fact that, two days previously, we had used a hose pipe to spruce up the small area just outside our front door. The water, which had been just enough to wash down four square feet of terracotta tiling, had descended the twenty five steps between our home and the driveway before turning right, and then right again, and had climbed a step that stood about three quarters of a foot high, before making its way south, skipping over a doormat, and soaking the Guppys' hallway carpet. The carpet, which was apparently made from pure wool, needed to be replaced, and the old man went on to insist that, as he and his wife would be forced to stay in a hotel until replacement flooring was fitted, we should also fork out enough hard cash to provide accommodation and meals for a week. During the evening of the following day, after having had no response from us, another note was delivered. The old man wanted to know when he would be receiving our cheque.

Shortly after the arrival of the second note, a group of the old couple's supporters assembled on the driveway in view of our front door and, while Pat Guppy held up a small soaking wet rug and shook her head repeatedly, the congregation rallied sympathetically, and very audibly, and issued many dark and disapproving looks in the direction of our bedroom window. The rug, which appeared to be older than its owner, was paraded back and forth along the driveway, and then laid to rest with great pomp and ceremony onto the paving stones within the old couple's garden, amid sighs and declarations of 'it was a good rug' from all present. There was much back patting and a certain amount of hugging amongst the women and then, after making its way back towards the front of the drive, the group halted its progress and remained huddled at the foot of the stone steps which led up to our front door, discussing our foul treatment of the poor old couple, for more than half an hour.

'We should get up a petition,' Mr Axley suggested. 'Get them out of this place before they can cause any more bloody trouble.'

80

'Oh, you'd do that for us?' Pat Guppy asked, wiping a tear from her sodden cheek and placing one hand affectionately against Axley's arm. 'Oh, oh, we'd be so grateful. You don't know how we've suffered, you just don't know.'

'Come along now, don't get yourself in a state,' Mrs Palmer chimed in. 'They aren't worth it.'

All eyes turned to our window again.

'We'll have them out of there in no time, you mark my words,' Axley said, reassuringly. Several of those assembled got out their pens to demonstrate their willingness to sign whatever formal paperwork was soon to be drawn up.

'We're behind you Pat,' the departing mourners called out as they exited the driveway. 'You can count on us.'

The next day a couple of large onions landed inside our garden, and a tomato was launched onto the bonnet of our car as Roy pulled into the driveway. As we cleaned the car's windscreen and cleared away the rotting vegetables which had remained on the drive since the arrival of that first courgette, Pat Guppy stood less than ten feet away from me and telephoned the local Environmental Health Department to report us for leaving rubbish on the driveway and alongside the old pair's front door, complaining that this had begun to attract rats. And later that day, after the old woman had strewn a few potato peelings over the step in front of her front door and across the drive nearby, to replace the cauliflower fragments that we'd removed earlier, the Guppys called James Floyd over to take in the scene so that he could better appreciate the need to sign the hastily produced petition which was then thrust under his nose, and to insist that we were also leaving various bits of lettuce and the such like inside the old couple's garage in the middle of the night.

The old man went to great lengths to prove his claims over the following weeks. He would go to his garage late at night, under cover of darkness, to deposit a bag of potatoes or carrots for discovery the next day. Then, during the following morning when Floyd was there to witness events unfold, he would bring out handfuls of the chosen vegetable whilst exclaiming that he'd found them on the bonnet of his car, or underneath it, or behind one of his folded garden seats. He would emerge with a bundle of lettuce leaves and place them on the drive before photographing the arrangement, and then stand over them shaking his head and mumbling that we'd been at it again. When the odd Brussels sprout and a handful of garden peas didn't cause enough of a stir amongst the locals, he'd get out his car and head off down the street with several small gherkins attached to his windscreen wipers for effect. And not once did one single person question how we were able to gain access to a garage that was locked all day and all night. No. They simply shook their heads in disbelief, uttered some consolatory phrase to appease the old pair, and took out a pen to add their name to the long list of men and women who had already attested in ink to their desire for our hasty departure.

Groups of the faithful visited the Guppys' flat each and every day, to congregate in front of the old couple's home and talk at length about their disgust concerning our behaviour. They did so audibly whilst we were out of sight, but would fall silent and rush off in the direction of the street or into the Guppys' flat if we emerged into plain view. Having been informed previously that we were drug dealers who practised black magic, I imagine they believed we would gun them down or turn them into frogs if they remained long enough to catch our attention.

So, away they scurried at speed, to seek refuge behind the old pair's solid wooden front door, or onto the open road where the presence of eye-witnesses to any assault, whether by lethal weapon or thunderbolts and purple smoke, would deter us from striking them down.

By the middle of December the novelty was wearing off. There were fewer visitors to the scene of each incident, and a decrease in the number of sympathetic remarks or cries of outrage from those who did stop by, and the old man was forced to increase the quantities involved in the hope of greater dramatic effect. Nearby neighbours had begun to question whether perhaps the various fruit and vegetables, and the occasional meat or dairy products, that made their way onto the driveway by the Guppys' front door could have been thrown there by children who were playing a practical joke. This infuriated the old man, and drove him to hurl even larger amounts of produce onto a greater number of locations. There were tomatoes thrown in front of our garage and hurled onto the Guppys' own garden, and even our neighbour's tree suffered an aerial assault one afternoon when the old man, annoyed by the repeated implication that a disgruntled schoolboy had covered his doorstep in parsnip peelings and several pork sausages, launched half a carrot in the direction of James Floyd's windows, as he had been the instigator of the vicious and vexatious rumour, and missed by a mile.

But it is the nature of vegetable hurling that, whilst it is undoubtedly an inconvenience to the one at the receiving end due to the amount of sweeping up required, it is not considered threatening or sinister. It is considered foolish, and slightly entertaining. A man wielding a knife as he threatens you is very frightening indeed, but one wielding a honeydew melon is just slightly ridiculous and in danger of ruining a perfectly good fruit. And so, despite the increased amount of interest in the goings on at the property amongst the locals, the Guppys gained nothing in return for their effort and the large amount of money spent at the local greengrocer, and must have approached Christmas wondering if it had been worth the bother. A few squashed sausages were their last offering before they left to visit their children that year and, as the old pair departed, Pat Guppy criticised her husband loudly for having been so foolish as to throw out meat which was still well within its 'use by' date when there had been a perfectly good cabbage rotting in the larder. The sausages remained outside the old couple's door for the next couple of days, until they were removed by the Mrs Finch from across the road, who had been charged with guarding the flat in the Guppys' absence for fear that we would break into it and fill their bath with grapes.

The departure of the sausages signalled the beginning of a temporary cease-fire, and we enjoyed a fortnight of relative peace and quiet while the Guppys were away. That said, those two weeks were not entirely without incident. Mrs Finch, the old woman who had been put in charge of looking after the Guppys' flat, visited the property each morning and then again in the evening, but her duties in the old couple's absence weren't confined to checking that everything was turned off or on, watering the plants and feeding the cat. No. As Pat Guppy's chosen one, her obligations included the performance of certain tasks usually carried out by the old couple themselves on a daily basis. So, at ten o'clock sharp every morning she would appear on the pavement that ran alongside our garden, and stand behind the lilac tree, in the spot usually occupied by the old man. She would check the time before commencing and then stand perfectly still, aside from odd glances at her watch, whilst observing our bedroom window for a period not exceeding ten minutes. And just in case she was neglectful of her important duties, Pat Guppy's second chosen one, Violet Palmer from next door, was charged with making sure that Mrs Finch was in position at the correct time every morning, and that she didn't stray from that spot until she'd done a full ten minutes, regardless of the weather or a flare up of her arthritis. And so the old woman, dressed in a spotted raincoat and fur-topped ankle boots, stood outside in the driving rain under a red and white striped umbrella, watching our windows, while Violet Palmer stood watching her watching them.

CHAPTER FIVE

'I'M going to rip your head off, you bastard!'

The telephone rang at about half past six and Roy answered it. The stranger asked politely for Roy by name and then, after making sure that he was speaking to the correct person, issued the above threat.

The old couple had returned from their Christmas break a few days earlier, apparently rejuvenated and eager to pick up where they'd left off.

'Good afternoon' the old woman said as she passed Roy on the drive.

The old man sauntered along beside her, carrying his overcoat and grinning like a Cheshire cat. The dialogue between them was amicable, almost affectionate, and as they reached the entrance to their home the old woman turned to check that Roy was still within earshot before exclaiming: 'I am so happy to be home.'

Five minutes after crossing their threshold, the old woman was back outside. She approached Roy, who was just about to climb the steps to our flat, and informed him that the contents of the old pair's freezer had been ruined. Roy did not stop. He began his ascent and ignored her.

'Our electricity was switched off while we were away,' she said. 'Presumably by you.' She awaited a response and then, when none was forthcoming, continued. 'Our freezer was off for the best part of a day.'

Silence.

'It was full,' she said, raising her voice to enable it to travel across the growing divide between Roy and herself. 'There were numerous loins of pork.'

Roy opened the door to our flat and stepped inside.

'We had veal in there too,' she called out as Roy closed the front door.

A note appeared about five minutes later and then, roughly half an hour after it was delivered, an electrician from the local electricity board arrived at the property. He was taken to the cupboard beneath the stone steps and shown the electricity meters by Ben Guppy. The old man pointed out his meter, explained loudly that it had been tampered with by us, and indicated to the young man that the switch was in the 'off' position. The electrician examined the meter and told the old man that he could find nothing wrong with it, aside from it not being turned on. The old man looked flustered.

'I know there's nothing wrong with the blasted thing,' he said.

The electrician looked confused.

'I came home and found it this way.' He pointed to the switch again. 'What I want from you is a statement that you came here and saw it was turned off.'

'Eh?'

'Write it in your report that you came here and witnessed the electricity being off, on account of our neighbours who had tampered with the meter.'

'I can't do that,' the young man protested. 'I don't know who switched it off now do I. Could have been you for all I know.'

Ben Guppy positioned himself between the young man and his only available exit and repeated his requirements again, appearing to expect that the prospect of being trapped there with the old man for all time might elicit some alternative response. He explained that he was an elderly man, possibly because he thought his physical appearance didn't go far enough in revealing that fact, and informed the electrician that he was no longer able to climb a ladder or lift heavy boxes, and that his wife had angina and couldn't bend her left knee properly. The electrician was not swayed.

'I can't go doing that,' the young man explained. 'I'd get the sack.'

'Fuck off then!' was the old man's reply.

The following day, upon seeing our car pull into the driveway, Ben Guppy rushed out to meet us and, waving a blank piece of paper above his head, began chuntering on about the four hundred and eighty pounds we owed him for his ruined beef fillet steaks. He thrust the paper under Roy's nose and then whipped it away again, declaring as he did so that the note we had just been presented with was a sworn statement regarding the electricity meter, written by the electrician who had visited the previous day, confirming that we had been responsible for the spoiling of the old couple's food. Roy said nothing, which came as no surprise to the old man as silence was our standard response. Old man Guppy shook visibly as he waved the blank sheet around above his head, above Roy's head, and then stuffed it into his pocket. He hoisted a Tesco carrier bag into the air and displayed it for several seconds before speaking.

'Ten pork chops that will now have to be thrown away,' he said. 'Pay up...'

We headed in the direction of our home.

'Or else!' he concluded.

Roy stopped in his tracks, turned, and headed towards the old man. Ben Guppy took one step back, then another, and then another. Roy continued moving forward until the old man, placing one foot behind himself only to find that he had left the driveway behind and was treading on soft wet soil with his back only inches from the garden wall, came to a stop.

'Or else what?' Roy began, leaning in towards his adversary as the old man wriggled about and looked for an escape route. 'What will you do, eh? Tell the neighbours we're black magic practising drug dealers? Oh wait, you did that already.' Roy stepped closer, bringing himself to within five inches of the end of Ben Guppy's nose, and laughed. 'Do your worst old man.'

Ben Guppy, entirely taken aback by being addressed directly, stood in stunned silence. Pressed against the damp wall, with fronds of ivy tickling the top of his thinly covered cranium, he raised one leg in an attempt to prevent himself sinking any further into the moist sod, tilting slightly as the other failed to support his weight adequately. As Roy stepped back and turned to leave, the old man hopped sideways onto a pile of wood chippings, steadied himself, and awaited the opportunity to make a run for it. Observing Roy's progress, he took one tentative step towards the driveway, called out 'aha!' triumphantly to signal his escape, and fell arse over elbow onto the cold wet tarmac.

The following evening we received the telephone call I mentioned previously, from the stranger who was polite enough to make sure he was speaking to the intended recipient of his threat before delivering it. And the morning following the telephone call, as Roy stepped outside to take delivery of a parcel of books that I'd been expecting, Ben Guppy stood on the drive looking rather more pleased with himself than he had done the day before, when he'd been laid out on his back in more or less the same location, and called out to ask if either one of us had suffered a change of heart yet. He gestured, his hand forming the approximate shape of a telephone receiver as he placed it against the side of his head. 'Call me,' he said, laughing as he made his way indoors.

We'd been warned about the Guppys' less than desirable connections many times, so the surprising element to this particular development wasn't that it took place, but rather that it hadn't taken place sooner. The first call was short. The second call, received a day later, went into greater detail and involved references to Roy's head and his backside getting better acquainted with each other. The third caller, who rang at about seven in the evening a week or so after his predecessor, was a much older man. And when I say much older I mean closer in age to the Guppys themselves. He obviously wasn't a professional, and must have been hired to stand in for the usual young man who, presumably, had gone off sick at short notice. The third caller got off to a bad start, as he failed to remember the name of his intended victim and had to refer to his auto prompter, a muffled Ben Guppy, who offered directions audibly in the background. Back on cue, the stranger began his tirade of abuse, but before he could reach the end of his first sentence he ran out of change and was cut off. He did call back, but appeared to have lost some of the enthusiasm he'd summoned prior to his initial call, and after being criticised by his prompter for buggering it all up, told Roy to sod off and put the receiver down.

About half an hour or so later that Sunday evening, a fourth call came in, from a woman who identified herself as Mrs Lang.

'I'm calling on behalf of an employee of the local council,' she informed Roy. 'There have been some neighbour issues at your property and I've been asked to intervene. So can we arrange a time for me to visit you?' she asked.

'I'm sorry,' Roy said, 'who did you say you were calling on behalf of? Which employee of the council?'

'I can't remember her name right now,' Mrs Lang said, 'I'll have to check and get back to you. So, when can I visit to address Mrs Guppy's concerns?'

'Did Mrs Guppy ask you to call here?'

'No, she knows nothing about this,' Mrs Lang explained. 'I am calling in an official capacity.'

'Where did you get this number from?' Roy asked.

'It's on file at the council.'

'If I were to tell you that the number you've called has only ever been given to four people, two of which are Mr and Mrs Guppy, and that the remaining two are members of my wife's family, would you like to confirm again that you got this number from council records, and that Mrs Guppy didn't put you up to this?'

The line was silent.

'Did Mrs Guppy put you up to this?' Roy repeated.

'She asked a friend to call you,' Mrs Lang admitted, 'and that friend asked me.'

Despite that particular admission, however, Mrs Lang was in no hurry to cut the call short, and appeared to believe that her powers of persuasion were such that a visit could still be arranged and an amicable solution could be reached for all concerned if we were willing to put in the right amount of effort. A short call the following day, from an unnamed individual who sounded remarkably similar to threatening caller number three, confirmed our suspicions by informing us that by 'effort' Mrs Lang had in fact meant 'money.'

Several days passed and each evening we received another call, sometimes threatening, sometimes 'official'. After two weeks of being told that we were going to be beaten up, or taken to court for having a bath after eight in the evening, Roy instructed the telephone company to issue a new number and called the community police officer again, hoping that, unlike extortion and harassment, making malicious calls was considered by the local force to be an activity which violated the law of the land. WPC Purser was not interested in the threatening calls. She was, however, very upset by the number of complaints the old couple had made about our behaviour towards them during the weeks preceding and following the Christmas holiday.

'I have a file full of complaints about you,' she said accusingly. 'It's two inches thick. The complaints you've made about the Guppys only come to a third of that size.'

Roy explained that he didn't understand the significance of file size with regards to the legal justice system.

'A court takes one look at the size of the file against you and compares it to the one against the Guppys,' she snorted as she chortled. 'Your credibility would be shot.'

Roy explained that the Guppys could provide no evidence, and that we could provide a box full of the stuff.

'Evidence!' Purser exclaimed. 'We don't have time to go through all of that. It's your word against theirs, and like I said already, the file on you is thicker.' Her tone changed to one of mild ridicule. 'Anyway, they're just a couple of old people for God's sake.'

The old man appeared rather pleased with himself when the calls first started coming in. He strutted up and down the driveway like a proud peacock, and bragged loudly to his wife that he'd got a good deal when negotiating the cost of the menacing calls. The young man had wanted twenty five pounds, but old man Guppy had knocked him down to fifteen. He congratulated himself on having such excellent bargaining skills and a keen business sense, and the old woman got quite carried away as the two of them discussed the terror we must have experienced when the second caller threatened to beat us about the head with a cricket bat. After a week of calling, however, the strutting subsided. We came and went as usual, and appeared, outwardly at least, to be oblivious to the old couple's existence. Pat Guppy was outraged.

'What a waste of fifteen pounds,' she said to her husband, as she stood beside our car, examining the new hub caps. 'That could have been better spent on bread and milk.'

'It's early days yet,' the old man replied. 'Give it some time will you.'

'Time? Have you seen how much work they've had done to that car while we've been giving it time?'

The old man bent forward and tapped one of the caps.

'You can go without your pork pie at lunchtime,' the old woman said, 'as we're about to end up in the poor house. See how you like that!'

'If I'd denied you food every time you've behaved like an idiot,' he replied, 'you'd have starved to death years ago.'

For the next week they watched and waited, and waited and watched. They followed and photographed, and watched a bit more. And on the day that our telephone number was changed, having paid fifteen pounds for the privilege of seeing no noticeable difference in our behaviour whatsoever, the old man shot out of his flat like a bat out of hell, followed closely by a very red faced Pat Guppy, before being struck on the back of his head by a Tesco carrier bag filled with spoiled pork chops.

'I told you,' Ben Guppy screamed as he shuffled off down the drive towards the street. 'I'll sort it out!'

'You useless old fool,' the old woman called out, as she hobbled along behind him, arms outstretched as she attempted to grab the back of his collar.

'I'll sort...' He picked up speed as he hit the pavement and leapt out into the road, following the flow of traffic and attempting to keep up with a blue Nissan Micra. 'I'll sort it out!' He slipped between two parked cars and dashed past Mrs Palmer's front gate. "I have a plan!'

Bang, bang, bang. The old man's plan was put into action in the small hours of the following morning. Bang, bang, bang. The noise continued for about half a minute and then stopped. Then, as Roy had managed to get back to sleep and I was just beginning to settle down, bang, bang, bang. The sound of the old couple's pounding below continued on the hour, every hour, until six o'clock in the morning. And in between the loud thuds the old man yelled 'shut up!' at the top of his voice. We were treated to a repeat performance the next night, and the one after that, and every night for the following fortnight. And whilst we could ignore the majority of the Guppys' shenanigans during daylight hours, the sleep deprivation we were suffering we could not.

A quick telephone call to one Mrs James at the Environmental Health Department resulted in a letter being sent from her to the old couple to tell them to behave themselves in the wee small hours. Mrs James was not, however, of the impression that it would do much good, as we were the ones making all the noise. Ben Guppy was, apparently, a regular caller, both on the telephone and in person, and Mrs James knew all about the dog we kept chained up, barking at all hours, and the number of times we flushed our toilet after dark.

'We do not have a dog,' Roy explained. 'We have never had one.'

Mrs James wasn't convinced.

'One look at our home would confirm that,' he went on. 'There is no sign of doggy activity in here.'

'Why would Mr and Mrs Guppy make something like that up?' was Mrs James' response.

That was a question we encountered many times; a question which, judging by the tone in which it was delivered, seemed to suggest that the absence of a reason to lie was solid proof that no lie had been told. The more bizarre the untruth, and the more lacking in reason, the more certainty there was that it could not be a fabrication.

'I've been to Mr and Mrs Guppy's home several times,' Mrs James said, the sound of a smile in her voice suggesting that the image in her mind's eye was one of tea and crumpets and lengthy tales of copious fraternisations with the Deputy Mayor. 'I can't see how they would go about banging anything on their ceiling. Mr Guppy cannot climb a ladder you know.'

The old couple seemed more than capable of conjuring up unwavering belief in others, but they had ceased being able to do it between themselves. Increasingly paranoid and erratic, consistently offensive towards each other, less and less able to remember which lies they'd told to which person, and visibly confused that despite their best efforts they were still making no headway where we were concerned, the day to day strain of maintaining a facade of rational and respectable innocence, and of going without sleep every night just to make sure that we did the same, began to take its toll. Visibly overwhelmed by their desire to ruin us, and consumed by their failure to achieve the desired result, they continued to invest an ever increasing amount of time and energy into a failing plan that they were no longer able to define. They argued loudly throughout the day, and often in the middle of the night, and as the old man became less and less able to control his temper in public, his wife spent more and more time mopping up the resulting mess and trying to distance herself from his actions and their consequences. From the outset it had been the old man firing the gun, but we had never been in any doubt that the old woman had loaded each and every bullet. As time passed, however, her ability to control the monster she'd created diminished, until eventually the task was beyond her entirely.

Despite her obvious loss of control and increasing inability to get it back, Pat Guppy was a creature of habit who was entirely set in her ways. She could no more control what came out of her own mouth in the presence of the old man than she could control what came out of her husband's in the presence of strangers. When calm words and some expression of affection would have gone some way in quelling the old man's anger and possibly removed the likelihood of him rushing out onto the drive to threaten Roy with a good arse kicking, in full view of a visiting plumber, she was unable to offer it. She chose instead to remind Ben Guppy that, by failing to put either one of us in our place for more than a year, he had displayed a level of weakness which had confirmed the belief she had held since their marriage, that he was not a man. Having prodded the old man for decades to get him to do her bidding, she was unable to quit. And when Ben Guppy turned bright red and screamed at the top of his voice that he was going to kill Roy, one afternoon during the latter part of February, the old woman could not help but reply that he did not have the guts. Had she wanted him to prove her wrong? Perhaps. Had she wanted him to attempt to do it it in broad daylight with several witnesses present. Most likely not.

The old man's anger was due, for the most part on that particular day, to the rapidly decreasing size of his garden bush. The Guppys were thieves, and whilst trying in vain to get their hands on our money had decided to console themselves by stealing a sizeable strip of our land. Little by little their plants had wandered over onto our property. At first we put this down to their inadequacies as gardeners. They paid little attention to their flat's interior and even less to the exterior, so an unwillingness to tidy an overgrown garden came as little surprise. But as the months passed it became noticeable that, while he would trim certain parts of his garden every so often, the old man left that one section to continue growing unabated. Eventually, the invading bushes claimed more than four feet of land along the entire length of our property, and looked set to continue to five and beyond as we advanced towards the growing season. And in addition to cultivating his green troops as they marched on, the old man had driven stakes into the ground, tying lengths of string between them to indicate his new and improved boundary line before preparing to sink posts for a new fence. Believing that the old man was not at home, we considered it to be an ideal opportunity to set that one matter to rights at least, so Roy took a pair of garden shears to the offending bushes and reinstated the border between our property and that belonging to the Guppys.

But the old man had been home all along, and had witnessed Roy's chopping off of branches. He was furious. Believing it was very much against the law to assault your neighbour's bush without consent, he dashed out of his flat screaming, and waving his own pair of shears above his head.

'I'll kill you, you bastard!' he yelled, before heading off down the driveway towards the street in the direction of his parked car. Numerous failed attempts by the old man to put his gear into reverse, followed by an equal number of attempts to change into first as he manoeuvred in the road, were eventually followed by the appearance of his car at the entrance to the driveway. He paused, revving the small red vehicle's engine as he prepared to charge the driveway, in much the same way that a bull stamps at the ground and snorts as he prepares to gore the toreador. Then he hit the accelerator.

'stop!', Roy called out, as the distance between himself and the old man's car closed to just a few feet. And oddly the old man did.

Having realised his mistake, Ben Guppy, red faced and hot under the collar, struggled again to push his gear stick into reverse before slowly backing off down the driveway in preparation for a second attempt.

'Stay there!' he shouted at Roy, as his car reached the entrance to the drive and he attempted to bring it back into first gear. 'Don't move!'

He put his foot down. The sound of tyres spinning against tarmac filled the air, along with the acrid stench of burning rubber. The car shot forward, juddered, and slowed to a crawl. He scanned the drive and spotted Roy, who'd dashed to safety immediately following the old man's first attempt to run him down.

'Bastaaaaard!' Ben Guppy called out. 'Get back here!'

Then, realising that his orders weren't about to be obeyed, Ben Guppy clambered out of his car, rushed around to the front of the drive and onto the pavement beyond it, grabbed the first bag of rubbish he could lay his hands on, and attempted to sling it, with all his might, in Roy's direction. The bag, unfastened and full to brimming with the fish dinner he'd cooked a few nights earlier and a large amount of used kitty litter, was launched skyward at an unsatisfactory angle, rising in height but not travelling far in horizontal distance. Turning on its head at speed before beginning its descent, it regurgitated its contents, spewing cat droppings and decapitated cod heads in the old man's direction. Enraged, humiliated, purple-faced and suddenly rather pungent, the old man yelped, stamped his feet on the ground several times, and then ran screaming in the direction of his home, leaving his car, with door wide open, sitting on the drive.

The Ropers were in their garden that afternoon. Having seen everything that had taken place on the drive, they wasted no time in telling me so when our paths crossed the following morning. They were absolutely disgusted, or so they said, by the old man's behaviour, and Dave Roper had considered giving the old man a piece of his mind. Personally I doubted he could spare it. But in any case, the man was all hot air, and only fifteen minutes after offering his support, and his solemn word that he would put what he'd seen in writing for our solicitor, Roper was out on the drive with Pat Guppy, promising to put together an altogether different written version of events for her.

'We must help each other out,' the old woman said. 'It's what neighbours do.'

'Oh, I couldn't agree more,' Dave Roper replied.

'Yes,' Anne Roper chimed in. 'Yes, yes.'

'I mean, what was the foolish man thinking, rushing out in front of Ben's car without warning like that. He could have got himself killed,' Pat Guppy continued.

'Oh absolutely,' the Ropers sang out in harmonious accord.

There had been other witnesses that day, most of whom had stood at the foot of our steps several months earlier shouting insults and waving fingers. Oddly enough, all of them had suffered chronic short term memory loss by the following morning. And by the following evening the Ropers had followed their example and remembered that, at the time of that particular incident, they had in fact been somewhere else, doing something else, and had seen many people but definitely not Ben Guppy. No, not at all.

The old pair's most dedicated followers did not waver in their devotion. Those on the fringe, however, began to falter. Whilst they did not openly accuse the old couple of being at fault, for fear of reprisals as they were still under the impression that Pat Guppy had a direct line to God, they began to put some distance between themselves and the old pair. From that day forward, for a number of our neighbours, our latest exploits held much less interest, and few were so eager to console the old woman when she went to them crying because we'd kept her up all night long again. That's not to say that the locals' behaviour altered towards us, however, as they still held us accountable for the inconvenience they'd suffered due to our unwillingness to allow the old pair to run rough shod all over us and the Guppys' repeated and lengthy complaints regarding that fact. But the number gathered alongside our steps, the next time the old woman called for support in her hour of need, was halved, and those who did turn out to pat her on the back did so with much less enthusiasm.

In the days that followed, Ben Guppy returned home each evening, drunk as a skunk and barely able to make it to his front door. He shouted at his wife at all hours of the night and day, regardless of whether or not she was at home, and told the neighbours repeatedly that we had stolen his dustbin lid. In the search for that cherished circle of galvanised steel, without which his dustbin didn't feel complete, he scoured every inch of the drive, our garden, and then his own, before turning his attention to his garage and eventually ours. Unable to break down the door, despite several attempts to kick it in, a couple of which were made following a running jump, he picked up a boulder from his overgrown rockery and hurled it at the small window situated at the the top of one of the wooden doors. It missed, hitting the side of our garden shed and landing with a thud on the ground a few feet in front of him. Undeterred, he retrieved his trusty rock and launched it into the air. Thud. Then again. Thud. Then, having failed to knock a hole in anything, he rushed along the drive, arms flailing and head thrown back, kicking his legs out in front of him as he picked up speed. Heading for the steps that led up to our front door, but turning too late and overshooting the mark, he hurtled forward unable to stop, landing face down across the bonnet of our car. He lay there for a few seconds before beginning to pound his fits against the shiny silver surface, and then slowly slid sideways until he toppled over onto the drive.

Inspired into action by the old man's rock hurling and high speed antics along the drive, and concerned for the safety of our car, and also for ourselves at that point, we decided to seek out a replacement for Mrs Fairbanks. John Mayfield was the name of our new solicitor, from the firm of Swindle, Shaft and Grunt. He was a stern man who turned out, a few weeks after taking our case, to be very bad at listening, incapable of offering constructive advice, and very willing to take a fee whilst doing very little to deserve it. If he had been half as hostile and unsympathetic towards the Guppys as he became towards us then he would have been just the man for the job. Sadly he was not. But during initial discussions he seemed very knowledgeable and quite determined to bring about an end to our situation, and after he had acquired a basic understanding of our predicament, a very lengthy and rather aggressive letter was fired off to the old couple without delay.

CHAPTER SIX

AFTER being diagnosed with depression, by our good doctor Cranston, Roy and I were told that counselling would be immensely helpful in our situation, but as the government was raping the national health service and not providing the funds necessary to maintain the physical and mental health of the general populace, that anti-depressants alone would have to do. I spent the next pill-popping week feeling sick to my stomach. During the second week the nausea was joined by a feeling of elation, which meant that I still felt sick but didn't care about it so much. And during the third week I was granted total clarity.

Now, before I go on, I do want to make it clear that I am not suggesting that anti-depressant or their manufacturers are responsible for inducing a need to kill in the average female human being. That would be entirely misleading. But whereas the homicidal maniac usually feeds on a large amount of confusion, a cold-blooded killer like myself requires total clarity. And therefore, whilst not meaning to I'm sure, the wonder pills I popped each day opened up avenues I'd never previously considered exploring. And whilst clarity, by itself, wasn't sufficient to inspire enough confidence to enable me to end the old man's life, my altered perception of my situation, and that of those around me, was a vital first step towards retaking control of my life, and ultimately removing Ben Guppy from the face of the earth.

So, one sunny afternoon towards the end of June, caring little about the old woman standing on her step watching me, or the small congregation of elderly groupies which had formed around her only minutes after I'd first emerged from the flat and put on my thick gardening gloves, I went about weeding our garden and preparing the soil for planting. And as I thrust my blunt little hand fork into the hard soil, and the old woman and her band of merry old men and women stood watching, waiting for me to shrivel where I knelt or burst into tears under the pressure of their gaze, I began to whistle a merry tune which I had picked up from an old movie, regarding Hitler and the fact that he had only one ball. There was a lot of chattering behind me, and several comments about the lack of respect I was showing to a woman so much older than myself and so much more important. The old woman informed them that I would be sorry, and that they would see that all in good time. But as the old men and women dispersed and I prepared to begin my fourth rendition of that highly amusing melody, Pat Guppy, who appeared more than a little vexed by the volume I was able to achieve with just two puckered lips and a lot of puff, retreated back over her threshold and chose to watch me, for the remainder of the time I spent out there, from behind the safety of her front door.

So what had changed? What had forced the old woman to retreat into the shadows while her cronies looked on? Until that moment I had considered the change in me over the previous couple of weeks to be so slight as to be practically invisible to all but those who knew me intimately. But the old woman had seen it, and she'd been worried by it, and the more I thought about that the happier I felt. It cheered me up so much that I went out there again the following day, lips glossed and ready for making music.

I had been gardening for about an hour when the old man returned home. He didn't look surprised to see me there, no doubt having been given a highly detailed account of my brazen behaviour the previous day, and seemed a tad pleased in fact. Pat Guppy had been behind her front door from the moment I descended onto the drive. I knew this because she had been flicking her door catch constantly for about half an hour to demonstrate her presence. But upon the old man's return she emerged from behind the door and took up her usual position on the step in front of her home, with feet apart and arms folded, and prepared to bore a hole into the back of my neck with her eyes. The old man always preferred to bore a hole into my chest with his bloodshot and bespectacled baby blues, but I wasn't about to turn around and give him the opportunity. The old pair stood there for a few minutes, watching in silence, and then, as I shifted position and moved onto the drive to work on tidying up the edge of the border, Pat Guppy signalled to her husband to go inside with her. They were gone only a couple of minutes before returning, and it was plainly obvious, even in the absence of a salute and click of the boot heels, that the old man had been given his orders.

I didn't hear the sound of the old man's garage doors being flung open, the slamming of his car door, or the starting up of the car's engine, although these things must have taken place. I wasn't prepared for the appearance of the old man's car at the side of the building as I stood back to admire the progress I was making, and as the small red run-around headed straight for me I had little time to think, and even less opportunity to act. Moving sideways, but not quickly enough to put any great distance between me and the shiny red bonnet, the car missed me by a whisker. The surprise of having it come so close knocked me backwards and I landed awkwardly on top of the garden soil, twisting my ankle and bruising the side of my thigh. My tools suffered a worse fate. Having failed to hit me the old man forged ahead, ignoring the potential damage a pair of long-handled shears might do to the front of his vehicle, and ran them down mercilessly. As it happened, it was his back tail light which bore the consequences of our encounter that day, but this was not the result of one of the tools flying up into the air and hitting it as the car sped by. No. It was the result of me flying up into the air and hitting it with the blades of a heavy pair of garden shears as the car paused politely to allow the traffic to pass before pulling away onto the street.

The old woman was astonished and furious, and more than a little confused. Left standing there alone, in the presence of what she considered by then to be an obviously deranged lunatic, she didn't know whether to stay put and wait for her husband's return or rush indoors and let him take his chances with me. Faced with myself that day, I'd have opted for the safety of going indoors, but Pat Guppy was no genius so chose to stay put. I had never experienced such anger before. Tired and frustrated by the old pair's constant intrusions into our life and their relentless attempts to intimidate us, I had not had the energy to maintain such fury, but there on the drive that day every aggressive thought I should have had up until that point, and every inclination to kick back that I had suppressed for fear of making matters worse than they already were, emerged simultaneously and took hold of me.

Pat Guppy stood motionless on the step outside her front door. She looked past me in the direction of the road, perhaps for some sign that the old man had parked their car and was on his way back, or in the hope that some passer by or neighbour would come to her aid or send for the cavalry. But the old man was nowhere to be seen, and the street was empty. She seemed visibly relieved when I threw the shears onto the ground, but less so when I picked up the garden spade. As I approached her she stumbled backwards, grabbing for the first thing that came within reach. A small bag of rubbish had been hooked onto the handle of the old couple's front door and, in the absence of anything more threatening, she unhooked it and held it in front of her for a moment before tossing it directly at me. As the bag left her hands and made its way towards me she fled, and by the time it had hit me and rebounded onto the drive she was behind her door, whimpering and fumbling at the lock.

In truth I had no intention of bashing the old woman over the head with any of my garden tools, because there is a great difference between smashing in a tail light and smashing in a human skull. Apart from being incredibly averse to the sight of blood, whether my own or anyone else's, I had not reached the stage where taking a life seemed appropriate or necessary, and all I'd wanted to do that day was frighten the old woman. She had been the cause of so many sleepless nights for Roy and myself, and I wanted to give her a reason to lie awake, sweating profusely and jabbering in the dark, for the next couple. I'd done what I set out to do and returned home with a smile on my face.

The old man, of course, was more concerned for his tail light than he was for his wife, and returned to the building apparently more determined to put us in our place than he had been before. He screamed at the top of his voice that he was going to kill Roy, despite the fact that I had been the one who damaged his car, and hurled a box of old newspapers onto the drive at the foot of our steps to demonstrate the level of his anger.

'See how you like that!' he shouted, as he slammed the box against the ground.

He paced this way and that, and travelled the entire length of the drive on foot repeatedly for the next hour, stopping every now and then to check the street to see if Roy was about to return. He could not settle, and in response to the old woman's requests that he go indoors and stop making a fool of himself, he yelled at her again about his murderous intentions and the repercussions she would suffer if she didn't shut her mouth. I could have saved the old man the trouble of pacing and shouting and checking the street repeatedly, as I knew that Roy was going to be away that evening on business and wouldn't return until the following day, but there was something about the way the old man huffed and puffed and lost his balance every so often that I found entertaining. I'd never noticed it before, but the old man looked very small if you looked past the yelling and fist waving. And he looked old. Much older than he had looked when we first moved in.

At about eight o'clock that evening a police car pulled onto the drive, with lights flashing and sirens blazing, and two rapid response policemen climbed out of it. The old man rushed out to greet them, wringing his hands and gesturing towards his own front door. The men stood talking on the driveway for a few moments before they made their way to the street, to the spot where the old man's car was parked. One of the policemen examined the damage to the tail light. Then he examined the scratches to the side of the car which seemed to have appeared at some point between the old man racing off after trying to run me down and his eventual return to the building. As Ben Guppy paced back and forth, obviously in the throws of recounting the events of the day, although most likely dished up with copious amounts of dressing and a side order of curly fries, the two uniformed men stood silent. The air gained a slight chill. The old man went on. The temperature dropped a little more. He turned to face our flat, pointing towards our bedroom window and waving his finger about in an accusatory manner. The two men followed his gaze but examined the building only briefly before looking back at the old man.

'No!' Ben Guppy called out as the two officers began to make their way back to the squad car straddled across the drive. 'No, no, no! You don't understand!'

The two uniforms halted.

'No!' the old man repeated.

One of the uniforms took out a notebook and stood with pencil poised. He waited, watching the old man recoil. Moments later the policemen were gone, and Ben Guppy was left standing alone on the drive, shaking like a leaf and grasping the sides of his head with both hands.

I couldn't help but wonder why there had not been a knock at my door that evening. I had been prepared for it. The appearance of the policemen had been no great surprise, although the dramatic manner in which they'd arrived had taken me aback slightly. WPC Purser had repeated on more than one occasion that the word of a respectable couple like the Guppys was worth more than any amount of tangible evidence or any number of eye witness accounts, so I hadn't ruled out the possibility of spending the night in a cell. But the two men had departed without giving me so much as a second look, and I wanted to know why.

As it turned out I didn't have to wait long to find out. James Floyd, who had always insisted that he wanted to stay well out of things as he didn't want to take sides, had nonetheless continued to embroil himself in every aspect of the conflict by offering a friendly ear, which he claimed was impartial, to both the Guppys and ourselves, and had encouraged both parties to consider him their ally whilst claiming to be nobody's at all. He would offer some titbit of information or gossip, usually of a kind to make matters worse, feigning allegiance whilst attempting to glean details from us that could be passed on to the Guppys. And then, often not more than a minute after talking to Roy or myself, would be undergoing the same process with Ben Guppy or his wife. In addition to this, he was as changeable as the weather. On Monday he would insist that the Guppys' stories did not sound wholly unbelievable, and on Tuesday he would state quite emphatically that the old pair were clearly out of their minds. He was incredibly duplicitous, but had defended his position by stating that it was necessary for his own survival.

As the situation had deteriorated, however, the Guppys had called on him more and more frequently. The old man waited for him first thing in the morning so he could have a quiet word before Floyd went off to work. And when Floyd returned home he would often find Pat Guppy eagerly awaiting his arrival, ready with the latest news from the front line in her war against us, or with some favour to ask concerning the same thing. The stories had grown more and more outrageous. The favours had become less and less acceptable and considerably more bizarre. And the visits and telephone calls, sometimes very late at night or early in the morning, had increased in both frequency and length. So, having decided that the old couple were no longer of sound mind, and therefore a danger not just to us but to him also, Floyd had been forced to reconsider his policy of taking both sides whilst at the same time claiming to take neither, and had expressed a desire to assist us, with the understanding that we would keep what he told us to ourselves.

At about half past seven during the evening following my attack on Ben Guppy's tail light, the doorbell rang. Floyd wanted to express his surprise at what had taken place the previous day, and his growing concern for our safety considering the old couple's most recent allegations. He explained that the old pair had been making complaints to the local police for some time, and had accused us on more than one occasion of plotting to kill them. Their most recent allegation, regarding the tail light and numerous scratches to their car, had been accompanied by an accusation regarding the pouring of an oily liquid onto the area just outside their front door and our desire to see them slip and break their necks.

'A few of the neighbours are taking the Guppys' very seriously,' Floyd explained. 'They're convincing people around here that you're really trying to do away with them.'

He laughed at the thought. I did too, but not with the same level of conviction that would have been present just a couple of weeks earlier.

'They're serious about this you know. They want you banged up. Thing is,' he said, 'the new plod in charge isn't too impressed with them.'

He went on to explain that WPC Purser was no longer the guardian of the Guppys' two inch file of complaints. The file, which had grown in thickness to a whole three inches, had been added to during a number of long lunches at the old couple's flat, and the nature of the complaints, along with the manner in which they were collected by Purser, had caused those higher up in the chain of command to raise an eyebrow during the previous few weeks.

'Long and short of it,' Floyd said. 'Ben Guppy's been warned about dialling 999 when you two so much as fart near him, and Pat Guppy's contacts in the force have suggested she not attend the next police charity ball.' He paused, considering whether to divulge the remainder of the information passed on to him for safe keeping. 'They told Ben that if he makes one more official complaint they'll lock him up and...'

'But they still came out here yesterday,' Roy interrupted.

'Only because he got Violet Palmer from next door to 'phone it in. They told him if he wanted to take things further he could do it down at the station, from a police cell. Put the wind up him that did.'

The old couple's return to allegations of attempted murder came as no great surprise, and neither did our neighbours' willingness to believe them. The area we lived in was quiet and conservative, and populated predominantly by retired people with a lot of time on their hands. For the most part those who had at one time lived life in the fast lane had forgotten what it was like, along with the name of their cat and the place they'd left their glasses. The local currency was gossip, and the more scandalous its nature the higher its value. News of an attempted murder got you at least five invitations to coffee and biscuits, and news of several attempts got you afternoon tea, one slice of a layered sponge, and a three course meal followed by a selection of cheeses. The old couple had blackened our name and dined out on the proceeds. And that's what it was all about of course. The proceeds. Money, property, a free lunch. It was all the same to the old couple. They were determined to sink us, but they intended to rescue the precious cargo before the ship went down.

And in keeping with that spirit, a bill for one thousand, four hundred and sixty nine pounds dropped onto our doormat the morning following James Floyd's visit. Given that we already had around thirty bills from the old pair for one thing or another, we were used to receiving them by that time and the new arrival caused no great concern. Granted, it was the first bill to arrive for damage that one of us had actually had some part in causing, but we felt no differently than we had done upon receiving its predecessors. We simply added the newcomer to the pile and mentally moved on. The Guppys, however, were entering virgin territory. They were in a position where, for the very first time, the thing they were claiming had been damaged by us really did need to be fixed, and they were going to have to fork out the money to get the job done. The banging beneath our bedroom throughout the night had never ceased, but in the days that followed the arrival of that bill the pounding increased in both volume and frequency. Doors were slammed beneath us constantly, and the old couple's television set and radio were turned on full blast. The old man drove his car up and down the drive repeatedly, presumably to remind us of our obligation to pay for the damage he displayed every time he passed our windows, and when that didn't appear to be working he took to driving too close to our car, suggesting that the wing mirror could be his next victim, or manoeuvring his car over sections of our garden to exterminate the newly planted greenery.

Ben Guppy was bewildered. He was also more convinced than ever that the listening equipment present in his home was also secreted within the roof covering of his car, according to Dave Roper who, shortly before informing me that the old couple lived on pork pies as they'd been cleaned out financially by the cost of keeping Pat Guppy's invalid mother in a nursing home for years, assured me that he and Mrs Roper really weren't ones for titte-tattle.

'Lady Muck she is,' he continued, gesturing towards the old pair's flat and indicating that he was referring to Pat Guppy. 'Goes on about how she's descended from landed gentry because back in the Jurassic period her great great something-or-other was a lord. Thinks she owns the place, daft old mare. You should see the state of their flat.' He pursed his lips and drew in a deep breath. 'Filthy it is.'

'You were telling her about the daft sod and his devices,' Anne Roper said, nudging her husband.

'Oh, right. Yes. He was saying the other day, how he's been drilling small holes in his ceiling to find them. Daft sod. No luck so far.' He laughed, with one hand placed over his mouth to conceal his amusement from prying eyes. 'The car's next. He's already had a mechanic check under the bonnet, and since that was given the all clear he's talking about those listening devices of yours being buried in the lining in his roof. He's totally lost the plot.'

About five minutes later Pat Guppy made an entrance.

'Good afternoon Dave,' she called out. 'Such lovely weather for the time of year.'

'Oh yes Pat,' he replied. 'Very nice. And how are you today? Well, I hope.' He turned, his face concealed from her, and rolled his eyes. 'Bitch,' he whispered under his breath.

'Oh you know,' the old woman responded, 'mustn't grumble. I've been in town all morning.' She paused for effect. The volume of her voice increased, as did the level of pomposity, as she continued, 'doing charitable works.'

We'd heard a lot about the old woman's charitable works during the previous year or so. A veritable guardian angel to the sick and needy, Pat Guppy was incredibly proud of the fact that she was capable of sitting in the same room as members of the working class for five minutes at a time without gagging. A friend to every dilapidated building that served no purpose at all, she was regularly quoted in the newspaper as an authority on all things run down and useless. Always eager to support a good cause, she gave up countless hours of her precious time to attend free lunches and banquets with an open bar. And if a chairman was needed for a committee, the sole purpose of which was to discuss the forming of committees, she was the woman for the job.

Pat Guppy's good deeds formed the basis of the old couple's defence when a response was finally made to John Mayfield of Swindle, Shaft and Grunt. Apparently, it was inconceivable that a woman of advancing years, who devoted so much time and energy to eating and drinking her way to sainthood, whilst wearing an ugly frock, should be accused of harassing her neighbours. Did her friendship with the Mayor not provide enough proof of her good character, she wanted to know. It was an outrage of monstrous proportions, she asserted, that a woman descended from one of the noblest families in

Britain should be called to account for herself when, surely, the slightly watered down but almost blue blood in her veins set her above suspicion. No defence was offered for the old man as, according to his wife, his mere association with a person of her calibre should have placed him beyond reproach.

'We demand,' the letter concluded, 'that the invasive surveillance cameras which your clients have installed at the property be removed, as they invade our privacy and are an infringement upon our human rights.'

'Mr and Mrs Guppy are obviously mentally ill,' John Mayfield said. 'I informed them that the cameras will not come down. So, the best thing you can do now is to let them get on with it. Ignore them. I've done all I can do, so I suggest you get on with your lives and pray they don't live to see eighty. Anyway, they're just a couple of old people, how much damage can they do?'

'But, the letter you sent,' Roy protested, 'the threat of court action. We were serious when we said we were willing to go all the way with this.'

'Yes, well, I was not.'

And so ended our relationship with Swindle, Shaft and Grunt. The following day, angered by John Mayfield's insistence that we would not remove the bane of the old couple's existence, Ben Guppy took up a handful of damp soil from our garden and hurled it in the direction of one of the small black cameras, most likely in the hope that it would stick. Being twenty feet off the ground, the cameras remained clean and functioned perfectly regardless of the old man's repeated bombardments, and the only thing he got for his trouble was a sharp pain in his right shoulder that lasted for a fortnight and made it impossible to carry two full bags of shopping home from the supermarket at the same time.

With little else to fill his time, the old man paced and waved, waved and paced. And every so often he would stop and grin at the cameras. Or he'd pull out his tongue. But none of that made him feel any less frustrated or annoyed so, at nine o'clock in the morning on the first day of August, which happened to be a Monday, the old couple decided to mark the arrival of the new month by mooning, thankfully after adjusting their trousers but not their underpants, for the benefit of our CCTV cameras. The old woman, having bent double and directed her backside at the camera closest to our bedroom window, appeared to have some difficulty straightening up afterwards, and as her husband stood upright and dashed off in the direction of the entrance to the drive in order to greet the postman, Pat Guppy remained put, with her hands resting on her bent knees to stop herself from toppling forwards. After hearing his wife call out to him, the old man seemed undecided as to which was the most pressing matter, the erection of his wife or the ceremonial hand over of the morning's post. The post won.

The usual young man entered the drive from the left, after positioning his postal trolley alongside the stone gatepost, and Ben Guppy approached at speed on the right. Having no understanding of the concept of personal space, the old man continued on course, failing to stop as he came within a cat's whisker of the object of his fascination. He lunged forward towards the young man with arms outstretched. The postman, unsure as to whether old Guppy intended to hug him or grapple him to the ground, moved sideways quickly to avoid the collision, but the old fool continued on his original course at full speed

117

until he was deflected by the gate post and bounced out onto the street.

'Good morning,' old Guppy called out, as he tripped into the road and disappeared from sight.

Approaching the old woman, who had remained bent over double in the driveway, the postman greeted her cautiously before making his way up the stone steps to the first floor of the building to deliver our mail.

'I've mislaid a contact lens,' Pat Guppy explained, examining the young man through the tinted glass of her square-framed spectacles. 'I'm as blind as a bat without them'

Old man Guppy, having made his way back along the drive in time to witness the depositing of the mail, made some show of pushing bits of gravel this way and that in a searching motion with one of his feet. 'Daft woman,' he said, 'she's always dropping one.'

My mood at that particular point in time was philosophical. Admittedly, the old man's attentions towards us had been irritating and intrusive, but after almost two years of that sort of behaviour, and having a full bottle of wonder pills in my possession, it was rather like water off a duck's back most of the time. Well, it was for me anyway. One thing I had begun to notice was that Roy had not experienced the same metamorphoses that I had after the anti-depressants had begun to take effect. His thoughts did not seem clearer, his anxiety had not lessened, and far from feeling more able to cope with the presence of the old couple, he appeared to be more confused, more frustrated, and less able to come to terms with what was going on around him. He did seem a little more relaxed when he was at home, but he was just as anxious about leaving me alone as he had been before, and to a certain extent more so since the incident involving the old pair's car and my heavy pair of garden shears. He had made me promise that I would never do anything like that again because he felt I'd been reckless and had not considered the danger. He'd also made me promise that I wouldn't go wandering around outside when he was not at home because, despite the assertions of our neighbours, our solicitor, and the local police that Ben Guppy was just a deranged old man who posed no threat, he was nonetheless a malignant human being who seemed hell bent on running me over. I had no desire to add to the pressure Roy was under, or to make him feel any less able to look after me, so I made my promises, and at that point in time I really did intend to keep them.

CHAPTER SEVEN

IT was once believed that laurel endowed prophets with vision. I'm not sure it did that for Pat Guppy, and if anything, judging from her swaying to the left and right after having eaten a few leaves from the bush in her garden, it hindered her sight rather than improved it. But whatever it did, it ceased to do it at four o'clock in the afternoon on the fifteenth of August, 2005. It was then that we had apparently taken some form of toxic liquid and applied it to the leaves and roots of the old couple's beloved laurel bush in an attempt to poison them. We had done the same to their gooseberry bush according to the old man, and to their plum tree. As it happened I had no poison at my disposal, or at least I wasn't aware of having any if I did. But even if I had, it would hardly have been the most effective way to dispatch the old pair unless I knew for a fact that they would want plum or gooseberry crumble after their dinner each and every day of the week.

A group of well wishers congregated around the afflicted shrubbery at about half past four that afternoon and, judging by the bowed heads accompanied by the sombre period of quiet contemplation which followed the arrival of those called to the crime scene, a prayer was said for the bushes' survival. There was an awful lot of head shaking on the part of the congregation, and an equivalent amount of fist shaking on the part of the old man. He had turned a rather deep shade of purple and, standing there in his garden, his shiny little head could, from a distance, have been mistaken for the unusually large fruit of an extremely over active plum tree. The old woman held her head in her hands, and raised it only now and then to wipe a tear from her eye, while Mrs Palmer from next door offered a tissue and a shoulder to cry on.

As if the charge of mass planticide was not serious enough, we were also accused of moving around the contents of the old couple's garden. Plant pots had shifted this way or that, and the various containers and ornaments had been switched so that dwarf roses were where the chrysanthemums should have been and vice versa. The garden bench had been repositioned to give a reasonable view of the old couple's own garage doors, and a green plastic watering can had been placed upon it alongside a bag of potatoes and a potting fork. The discoloured plastic faux-plaster lion's head plaque which had always been given pride of place on the wall behind the garden bench had been turned upside down, and one of the assembly reminded those present that crucifixes are upturned to signify the presence of Satanists, so the upturned lion's head should be seen as signifying something very similar. By that time the black masses we were supposed to be holding every Sunday were notorious throughout the neighbourhood, so it was suggested by another of the congregation that one had taken place within the old couple's garden at midnight the night before. After raising every potted plant to investigate the bare slabs beneath, and discovering nothing, especially not the blood stains they had been expecting, the group concluded that there was no pressing urgency in calling in a priest to conduct a ritual blessing or exorcism. But to be on the safe side all present bowed their heads for a minute or so before leaving.

Letters started arriving in the post a couple of days later. The first few were very polite, asked us to reconsider our treatment of the poor old Guppys, and were supposedly written by concerned local residents. The few that followed after that asked if we had considered the precarious position we were putting ourselves in by treating such highly respected members of the local community in such a disrespectful manner, and each of those was apparently sent from a person connected with the local council. A few asked us to give some serious thought to the handicaps suffered by the old pair and their financial situation, and one suggested some sort of compromise regarding the amount of money we owed the Guppys and touched on the idea of an easy repayment scheme. None addressed us by name directly, and each one was unsigned, and we received one a day, every day, for a couple of weeks, after which time they began coming in pairs. As the days passed the tone of the letters deteriorated, and the last few we received reflected on the fact that such a prolonged period of conflict would most certainly prove to be extremely damaging for our health.

It wasn't the contents of each letter that caused me concern, or the sender's identity for that matter. It was Roy's preoccupation with both which worried me. For me the letters were nothing more than a minor aggravation and I indicated as much each time one was deposited through our letterbox. But Roy examined the contents of each letter at length, questioning the writer's motivation and hypothesising about what would most likely be contained within the next one. Convinced that the old pair were succeeding in their attempts to drum up local support, frustrated at our own failure to secure any assistance, annoyed by the apparent lack of justice in both, and finally succumbing to the old woman's numerous claims regarding her far reaching influence and her friendship with everyone who lived within a ten mile radius of our home, he was becoming increasingly suspicious of every local man or woman who so much as glanced in his direction. Despite the fact that, even if the old woman had really managed to muster the desired amount of support, we had done nothing to warrant the local council's attention and therefore had no reason to fear it, he talked repeatedly of precautions he believed we should take to protect ourselves, without having a clue as to what we should be guarding against. The fact that the handwriting in each of the notes bore more than a passing resemblance to that contained within the old man's numerous bills and demands for money went no way in convincing him that the only people truly obsessed with our downfall were the old couple themselves. And as the days passed, and the number of notes to examine and discuss grew, I watched as Roy crumbled under the strain of relentless and exhausting conflict.

I insisted with the arrival of each note that I was not affected, and attempted to persuade Roy that the situation was not hopeless, mostly without success, in the hope that it would not be too long before the old pair lost interest and moved onto something new. The Guppys, being compulsive creatures of habit, could not follow one course for long whilst receiving no reaction from us without growing increasingly impatient and being forced to rethink their strategy. True, they would return to each failed plot at a later date, so no course was ever entirely abandoned, but they would pull off the road for a time and explore new territory before rejoining it again when their new direction proved equally unproductive. So, when the letters yielded absolutely no reward whatsoever, they did stop arriving. We breathed a sigh of relief, for entirely different reasons, and were granted five minutes to collect our thoughts and assess the events of the previous few weeks before the personal visits began.

Our first visitor was the husband of Mrs Finch from across the road, who claimed to be the representative for our local neighbourhood watch scheme. He was an unsightly man, who wore the same jumper day in and day out, throughout the winter, spring, summer and autumn of each year, and whatever brand of aftershave he might have used it appeared to me that one of the most noticeable ingredients was definitely a breed of fish. He grimaced while he spoke, although I imagine the desired facial expression was more akin to a smile. And he wanted to come inside and speak to us at length about crime in the area. As it turned out it was our crimes he wished to discuss, the ones carried out against our neighbours, and he was none too pleased at being forced to do so on our doorstep rather than in the comfort of our living room. He was sent away empty handed, and as a punishment his wife was demoted from Pat Guppy's second in command to her third the following day, with Mrs Palmer rising up a level and taking over Mrs Finch's duties.

Our second visitor was an elderly woman who we had never set eyes on before, although she apparently knew everything there was to know about us. Much like Mrs Finch's husband, the elderly woman was not terribly impressed with being refused entry and having to give us a piece of her mind while standing on our doorstep. She was even less impressed with having to address our front door after it was slammed in front of her. It did not seem to deter her to any great extent though, and she continued to converse with it for ten minutes after we had gone inside and started making our dinner. She called out repeatedly, asking us to open up and let her inside, whilst hanging on to her umbrella as the rain poured down all around her. A strong gust of wind caught the underneath of her brolly and sent it flying off down the steps and across the drive and, after pausing just long enough to call out to us that we would rot in hell for what we were doing, the old woman followed after it with her raincoat flapping madly behind her.

I do not know who our third and fourth visitors were. In an attempt to avoid any further confrontations with the old couple's deranged groupies, we had decided not to answer our door if the caller was more than fifty years old and, despite pleas issued through our letterbox to open up and cease being so downright rude and ignorant, we were determined not to engage in any sort of conversation about the old couple with complete strangers who wanted only to further the Guppys' cause and insult us to our face at the same time. The callers persisted at all times of the day and night, and in all weathers, and most of those who were turned away came back repeatedly before finally giving up.

As the vexed visitors stopped arriving, small to medium-size parcels wrapped in brown paper and tied with old string took their place. In fact, nineteen such packets did. Having returned home from a few days away to find a pile of little red cards from the post office lying on our doormat, announcing a number of deliveries which had been attempted in our absence, Roy headed off to the post office to collect the sack of brown boxes, returning just fifteen minutes later, at about quarter to six in the evening. The first packet to be opened contained seafood which was well past its 'sell by' date. Opening the second revealed a dead and decomposing mouse. The third parcel contained the product of a large dog whose obviously unhealthy diet should have been addressed without delay, and unwrapping the fourth packet revealed the product of a similar animal, or possibly the same one, but in a much lesser quantity. As the wrapping and addressing of every one of the packets was almost identical, I saw no point in delving further into those that remained unopened, and each plastic box and its contents was thrown into a large black garbage bag at some considerable speed.

The old couple may not have heard our car pull onto the driveway as Roy arrived home, and they may not have seen him climb out of it and make his way up the stone steps to our front door when he returned from the post office that day. They could not, however, have missed hearing him shout at the top of his voice when we were confronted by the foul smelling contents of those packages. Roy descended the steps at speed, clutching the black plastic bag, before tearing it open and emptying its entire contents onto the step in front of the old couple's door. The old man, having ascertained that it was indeed Roy who was outside his portal, and that the seafood and droppings had accompanied him, rushed to open his front door with camera in hand, fumbled around with its casing before finally releasing it and positioning himself in the best spot for a half way decent shot, and then pressed its button. The old man's flash failed to go off as he endeavoured to capture an image of Roy standing alongside a pile of scattered animal excrement and decomposing shellfish, and he cursed the failing light and Roy's refusal to stand still while he went and got fresh batteries.

'I've had enough of this nonsense,' Ben Guppy shouted at the top of his voice, with face contorted and fists flailing madly. 'I'll have you!'

The old man rushed back and forth, kicking at the excrement and propelling a large portion of it onto the mat behind his own front door as his wife emerged and threatened to shoo Roy off the drive with an old balding broom. She caught the back of the old man's legs with the brush and, not recognising her mistake or being undeterred by it, pushed hard as she lunged forward.

'If you don't get out of here I'll break this over your back!' she screamed, yanking at the broom's handle and withdrawing it from the back of her husband's legs.

As the old man fell to his knees, crushing several prawns and cutting the palm of his hand on the sharp edge of a broken muscle shell, she pulled the brush from the end of the wooden broomstick and hurled it in Roy's direction, missing him by a few inches. The brush was followed by several lumps of flying faeces, which had been picked up off the drive after having been kicked into position by the old man, and the sound of both Guppys yelping, one in pain and the other with excitement.

I'm sure that, had the old woman not taken to tossing lumps of dog excrement at Roy's head, he would have come away content at having simply returned the old couple's property to them. He would most likely have considered that to be an end to the matter to a certain extent, as there was little else he could do to show his disgust or to punish the old pair for their consistently obnoxious behaviour. But the faeces was flying this way and that and, not surprisingly as the old pair appeared never to take into consideration the disadvantage they might possibly suffer in a confrontation due to the difference in physical strength between a young man and an old man or woman, they remained on the drive, shouting and waving their arms about. The old woman did appear to perceive some change in the wind, and began to retreat towards the open door to their flat as Roy stopped dead and headed back towards her, but the old man, still on his knees, continued shouting about his intention to see us ruined by Christmas. It must have come as some surprise to Ben Guppy as he felt Roy's open palm make contact with the back of his head, and he must have suffered some discomfort as he found himself face down on the drive with his hands pinned firmly behind his back. I wondered at the time if he saw any portion of his life flash before his eyes as his face was held against the gravel and pushed down hard. But judging by the old man's continued shouts of defiance and the old woman's jumping up and down while she called to her husband to wipe the floor with his opponent, I somehow doubt it. And Ben Guppy was still shouting at the top of his voice as Roy raised his fist and prepared to bring it down upon the old man's skull.

'Roy, stop!' I called out.

And he did.

Now, please don't read into my actions any desire to save the old man's skin. My only reason for stepping in when I did was to prevent my husband landing himself in jail. Whatever I might have thought constituted the perfect crime back then, I most certainly didn't think it included a spontaneous head battering that left finger prints, blood, hairs, fibres, and an infinite number of other clues scattered around the drive and the old man's corpse. So, Ben Guppy narrowly escaped being beaten to death, or at the least to within an inch of his life, although he was oblivious to the fact at the time. As soon as Roy released his hold, the old man lifted up his head, his face dirty and bleeding, and continued the tirade of abuse he'd been engaged in delivering just moments earlier. His wife, who had continued calling out to her husband to give Roy a good hiding, went from punching the air to clapping enthusiastically as the old man attempted to raise himself to his knees. She whooped, cooed, and giggled as she watched wide-eyed and full of hopeful expectation. Then she eeped, sighed, and chastised as the old man slumped forward and landed face down on the tarmac.

'Get up you old fool,' she insisted. 'Get up. Get up. Get up now!'

Pat Guppy dashed forward as Roy retreated. She took some time to bend down to a level where her hand could make contact with the old man's collar, and when she arrived in that position she grabbed hold of it, yanking hard.

'Get up now,' she continued, tugging repeatedly, 'or I'll never say another word to you for as long as I live.'

Ben Guppy, who had stirred a little and appeared to be summoning the energy to make a second attempt at pushing himself up onto his knees, thought better of it and, upon hearing his wife's final words, seemed to feel that staying put would be more beneficial under the circumstances.

Picking up the broom handle, which had been thrown onto the drive shortly after the launch of its brush and just prior to the first sizeable handful of animal excrement took flight, the old woman began poking her husband in the back. She prodded repeatedly, and he grunted an equivalent number of times but did not move from his horizontal position. 'He's getting away,' she warned, as she watched Roy head back towards the steps and then begin to head for home, 'do something you useless old fool!' She kicked at the old man's backside, grumbling to herself about the number of years she'd wasted on a man who'd been a liar and idiot since the moment he'd slipped that thin gold band onto her finger.

'You've never been any good,' she screamed. 'My mother was against me ever marrying you, and she was right. Even your own children can't stand the sight of you!'

Raising the slender length of wood above her head and preparing to bring it down across her husband's back, the old woman let out a shrill cry and then, spotting a slender uniformed policeman at the entrance to the driveway, she stood, as if frozen in time, with eyes wide and mouth open before snapping back into action.

'Arrest that man!' she exclaimed. 'My husband was taking the rubbish out and Mr Leah from upstairs assaulted him.' She pointed towards the top of the steps, where Roy and I had been preparing to go indoors. 'He's black and blue, just look at his poor face. He's just a poor old man.' She looked towards Roy and cried out 'why, oh why would you do this to a defenceless old man? What did he ever do to you?' before beginning to sob tearlessly.

The policeman glanced towards us and then walked towards the old couple.

'Come along now madam,' he said calmly. 'Drop the weapon.'

'Wha...' Pat Guppy looked up. 'This? It's just a broom,' she said incredulously.

'Which you were about to use to inflict serious bodily harm upon the gentleman laid out before you, who I assume is your husband,' he glanced at his note pad before continuing, 'Mr Benjamin Guppy?'

'No!' the old man replied.

'You're not Mr Guppy?'

'I mean no, she wasn't going to hit me, she was defending me against him! He came at me with a machete!'

'A machete?' the policeman echoed.

'A machete,' Pat Guppy confirmed.

'And where is this... machete?'

The old couple stood silent. Ben Guppy looked skyward for a moment for inspiration and then responded. 'He threw it in the bushes.'

'Have you been drinking sir?' the policeman asked.

The old man made no response.

The young policeman gestured towards the old couple's front door. 'Let's go inside, shall we?'

The assault which the old couple had conspired to provoke or invent for so long had taken place. The old man could offer not just his word, which WPC Purser had insisted was enough in and of itself, but also cuts and bruises as evidence to support his allegations. But the inevitable knock on the door from the uniformed young man, followed by a trip to the station and an overnight stay in a cell, turned out not to be so inevitable after all. As a small group of curious onlookers gathered on the opposite side of our garden wall, in a spot perfectly situated to see right into the Guppys' hallway, the policeman exited the old pair's home, signalling to those assembled nearby that there was nothing to see, and departed.

The following day there was an almighty commotion on the drive as Mrs Finch from across the road arrived with Mrs

Palmer from next door. Pat Guppy flew out of the flat below us, at a speed I had never seen her achieve in all the time I'd lived above her, and headed directly for her visitors. She called Mrs Palmer to her side, and the woman was as obedient and obliging as ever, leaving Mrs Finch standing isolated. Pat Guppy shouted and swore, criticised and chastised, and then shouted and swore some more. The object of her hostile attentions attempted some response but was silenced, as Mrs Palmer added her own criticisms to Pat Guppy's and attempted to match the latter's volume. As Ben Guppy joined his wife on the drive, the number shifted to three against one, and as Mr Axley approached, followed by his wife, it looked set to rise further still.

'I thought I was doing you a good turn calling the police,' Mrs Finch protested. 'I saw those two,' she gestured towards the first floor, 'and I thought, well... you've been waiting for your chance, and there it was!'

The assembled crowd jeered, making their disapproval evident.

'How was I to know they'd show up while you were...'

'You've done it this time Ada Finch,' Pat Guppy interrupted. 'You are not welcome here. You are not welcome in this street.' She paused, crossed her arms, and waited for her allies to follow her example. 'You are not welcome in this town.'

Mrs Finch's continued protests fell on deaf ears. The gathering turned its back on her and proceeded to ignore her very existence. She loitered a few moments, hoping to catch a glimpse of one friendly face amongst the number who had been her friends for the past ten or more years. Then, moving steadily backwards whilst still monitoring the crowd to see if one solitary soul would have the courage to break ranks, she made her way towards the driveway's exit. Forty-eight hours later a sign was erected at the entrance to her garden. It said 'for sale.'

There was an awful lot of cooing and flapping around the old couple following Ben Guppy's brush with death. Much was made of the nature of the attack, with some accounts having Roy chase the old man along the street before tackling him to the ground and dragging him, face down, up and down the drive for half an hour. Some claimed that they'd heard the old man's screams for help from half a mile away, while others insisted that he had stoically resisted any urge to call for assistance and had retained his dignity despite being bounced on his head repeatedly in full view of his wife, who had suffered a mild stroke and much palpitating in the chest region. The old man wore his battle scars proudly and paraded them regularly. And, far from being dissuaded from provoking his attacker again for fear of receiving some of the same, or maybe worse, the old man appeared entirely oblivious to the fact that he could actually have been killed and, if anything, seemed even more willing to place himself in precarious situations with increasing regularity.

The Guppys had been catapulted into the public spotlight by Roy's attack on the old man, and they liked being nowhere better. I think it's true to say that for a few weeks following that evening the old pair did inspire an increased amount of sympathy and concern amongst those living nearby, and the number of transient supporters did rise for a short time. But the hardcore malignant collective which seemed to continually hover around the old pair, possibly out of concern for their own image as a force to be reckoned with and fear that they would be seen as vulnerable by those who sought to oppose them, took offence at the idea of the old man being painted as the victim, and began to retell the story to all who'd listen with a number of important changes. Most significantly, Ben Guppy was depicted as the defiant under dog who rose up, rather like David, and brought his opponent, who was ten times his size, down with one blow to the head. This, of course, did not quite tally with the old woman's version which had him lying in a pool of his own blood for over an hour while Roy pummelled the back of his head mercilessly with a house brick. Inconsistencies and over embellishments rendered the story incoherent and unbelievable, and by the time the bruises had disappeared from the old man's face most of the locals who had voiced concern or support initially were questioning whether the old man might simply have fallen and injured himself, and only a little while later the idea that Roy had even been present had been dismissed entirely by all except those who were immovably devoted in their dedication to the old pair.

Having been visibly put out by the reduced amount of interest in their ordeal less than a month after it had taken place, the old pair were incredibly pleased when Pat Guppy's mother died. There is nothing quite like a funeral to stir up local interest, and the steady stream of concerned callers which had dwindled and then ground to a halt only a week or so prior to the old lady's passing, as the assault had been relegated to the old news archive, doubled in size during the few days prior to the funeral and more than tripled following the old lady's cremation. And the whole family had travelled from far and wide to be present at the event, so there were at least five more supporters on the drive following the funeral, as the old couple demonstrated their sadness at the loss of a much loved family member by pointing their fingers at the CCTV cameras, examining our car, shouting at our windows, and walking over our garden. The old couple's son-in-law, who was remarkably similar in appearance to the old man despite not being a blood relation, and had achieved an equivalent level of stupidity, devoted himself to pacing the perimeter of the property and examining any object even remotely connected with us, such as our steps, our front door, and our drain pipe. He did little else, and after having satisfied himself that there was nothing more to see, that his disgust at our existence had been adequately demonstrated in front of the CCTV cameras, and that we weren't about to do him the courtesy of exiting our home to allow him the opportunity of being disgusted to our faces, changed his clothes, rounded up his family, and went on his way. At some point I imagine that the group did leave the property and attend the old lady's cremation, but as the drive was not entirely emptied of mourners at any time that day there was no way of being certain of that fact.

Apart from affording the Guppys a further fortnight of fame, the old lady's passing had resulted in the inheritance of a small amount of money. The old couple enjoyed two pork pies for lunch instead of one for more than a month, according to Ben Guppy who announced the news to Mrs Palmer over the garden fence. The old woman bought a new coat, and the old man got drunk almost every evening for a week. As high as a kite, and even less in control of his senses and bodily functions than usual, he clocked up several hours, albeit in sittings of half an hour or so, lying prostrate on the ground in front of his home, and the old woman spent an even greater number of hours punishing him for it by means of continuous and immensely audible aggressive verbal assaults. Driven out of his home by the increasing volume of his wife's brow beating, the old man resorted to driving up and down the road in his car, narrowly missing other vehicles and coming to a full stop every so often as he fell asleep at the wheel. It was not unusual for him to leave his car parked across the entrance to the drive, with the keys still in the ignition and the driver's door wide open, while he staggered this way and that on his way to our garden wall, and the sight of him urinating against that structure became all too common. Of course, Ben Guppy did not need to be drunk to urinate publicly. In fact, he did not need to be urinating to take out what passed for his manhood and wave it at a wall or other similar structure. And his desire to expose himself to the elements was not confined to the presence of inanimate objects. No, indeed. He produced himself for my personal inspection on more than one occasion, and several of the neighbourhood's younger residents were unlucky enough to receive the same privilege. Always more impressed with the goods on display than any member of his audience, he seemed to think nothing of sitting inside his car as it was parked alongside the building, with his little friend resting in his lap, while he monitored young boys and girls making their way to and from school. For Ben Guppy, feeling the cool breeze waft around his particulars whilst he sat in his little red car, knocking back another bottle of cheap whisky, was one of life's greatest pleasures. He sat and fiddled, and giggled and observed, enjoying every moment as if it were his last, while I sat and contemplated, and considered and plotted ways to facilitate it being just that.

CHAPTER EIGHT

'PAY them, or pay the undertaker to bury your wife.'
A tall and rather well built scruffy-looking man in his forties appeared at the entrance to the drive, with arms outstretched, and brought Roy to a sudden halt, barring his entry to the street. The nature of the words spoken, and the time taken to confirm what had been said and grasp its meaning, left Roy speechless and motionless for just a few moments as he attempted to collect his thoughts and draw some conclusion regarding the most sensible course of action under the circumstances. But that pause, coupled with the distraction caused by my arrival at the scene and a subsequent shift in the focus of his attention, precipitated a delay which enabled the scruffy stranger to walk the few steps necessary to reach the old couple's car and climb into it, and for the car to then depart, before Roy had a chance to react.

If the old couple's intention had been to frighten us, then they had succeeded, and the serious concern we felt was doubled following a very similar encounter a couple of days later, this time late at night and with the addition of two more men and a sharp blade. However, if they had wanted to drive home the message that the only option available to us, if we wished to remain alive and kicking, or at least if I did, was to pay them whatever money they demanded whenever they demanded it, then they had failed. There existed another possibility, not altogether ideal but present nonetheless. The thought, though present for some time, had existed only in the realms of fantasy, as something to idly contemplate whenever the old man jeered and sneered and watched and threatened. It had remained caged. But following the appearance of the three hired thugs, and the smug grins on the old couples' faces, accompanied more often than not by loud hoots and a certain amount of hand clapping, the thought was allowed to sprout wings. It was allowed to take flight. Ben Guppy had got to go.

The old pair, being so regular in their habits, were predictable when it came to their comings and goings at the property. The old woman left to pursue her course to sainthood, and by that I am referring to her dedication to the countless charitable works she inflicted upon the local population whether they liked it or not, at the same time every morning. She returned for her lunch, preceded by the old man who rarely walked alongside her, and remained indoors for no more than an hour and a half before exiting the property again. She was home by half past four, and that gave her just enough time to have her dinner before leaving with her clipboard for an evening of after hours committee meetings, or whatever it is that self righteous condescending nobodies do after dark. She returned home at varying times depending on the time of year, but during the month of October she was always home by nine o'clock. Once indoors, she did not emerge again until the following day. The old man, however, took his time as he drove his car to his garage and locked it up for the night, and strolled back along the drive at a slow pace, stopping for a moment to survey the contents of his garden before making his way, at snail pace, to his front door.

There was only one area of the property which was dark enough, and adequately concealed, to enable me to remain unseen until my prey, oblivious to my presence and therefore unprepared, was directly in front of me and without any means of escape. That small area lay beneath the steps to the first floor, right opposite the old pair's front door. And the old couple, wishing to save on electricity, had long since stopped leaving the light on by the entrance to their home. The small storage room which was nestled beneath those steps, with its matt black door and complete absence of light, was the perfect place to lay in wait until the old man returned home, so I decided to hide there at the next available opportunity and await my chance to do away with him swiftly and silently.

Of course that was easier said than done. The old woman, who had been extremely reliable in her time keeping up until that point, left her meetings early for several days following the formulation of my hastily drawn up plan, and threw the schedule for my attack entirely out of whack. Then there was my own non-violent disposition to consider. Even my wonder pills only went so far in providing the necessary strength and confidence needed for the job, and I had not received anywhere near the necessary training for the task in hand. Then, just as Pat Guppy's routine returned to its previously predictable state, with her husband's therefore following suit, she came down with the flu and put pay to my plans for an entire fortnight. And a couple of weeks was just the right amount of time to facilitate the creeping in of doubt, so a third week passed while I struggled with my conscience, which had suddenly gained an independent voice, and contemplated an alternative course of action.

As I lay in bed cogitating, the sound of Ben Guppy clucking like a chicken drew my attention towards our bedroom window. He was strutting up and down the drive with his elbows stuck out, his head juddering back and forth as he impersonated an overly excited elderly cock.

'Puck, puck, puckaaaaaaaw,' he squawked loudly, 'puck, puck, puckaaaaaaaaaaaaaaaw!'

To his right, covered from top to bottom with broken eggshells and their exposed contents, was our car. There were broken pieces of creamy white shell attached to the windscreen wipers and aerial, and the top of the car was smeared with broken sunshine-yellow yolks. Congealed egg whites covered the front lights, and the sticky mess had slithered down the sides of the car and formed almost translucent puddles of golden slime on the driveway. Any projectiles which had failed to hit our vehicle had hit our neighbour's fence behind it or the very bottom of our steps, mingling with the milk which had spilled out from several broken glass bottles and the contents of two large torn boxes of table salt. Swirls of yellow and white mingled nearby the old man's feet, puddling around two discarded onions and threatening to form the basis of an omelette recipe. My conscience fell silent.

The first thing I needed was an adequate disguise. Firstly, I wanted to be perceived as a male, as that would throw suspicion away from me if I were spotted in the act. Secondly, I wanted to appear taller and more well built, as I didn't consider my actual physical size to be immensely threatening and it was a dead give away as to my sex. Boots with elevated heels solved the height problem, and the stuffing from a couple of pillows added pounds to my figure and broadened my shoulders. Binding my chest was necessary of course, as my newly created male physique was not rotund enough to explain the existence of an ample bosom. And a black wooly hat covered my long hair and concealed its colouring. Having gained three stones by the end of my endeavours, and about four inches in height, I found Roy's clothes to be only a little too large, and discovered that if I wore three tee-shirts under his black sweater I filled it out adequately. His trousers were not so easy to fill, but half an hour of loose tacking to the hems and a couple of extra holes in his belt meant that they stayed up and sat comfortably over my boots. It seemed doubtful that old Guppy would pay very much attention to his attacker's crotch area when faced with a well built man brandishing some form of lethal weaponry in a dark corner late at night, but he had expressed some interest in Roy's genital area when they were on speaking terms, much the same as he had done regarding my chest, so to be on the safe side and in keeping with the spirit of things, and giving due consideration to the possibility that I may have felt more inclined to act like a man if I felt more like one, I donned my husband's underpants and filled out the front with one of his socks, in case I failed in my murderous attempt and the old man lived to give a statement to the local police. My hands, being fairly small and slender, were too obviously those of a woman, so a pair of thick gloves were needed, and considering the fact that the numerous pairs I owned were all fingerless mittens in varying shades of pink, bright green or pale blue, or a combination of those colours with random threads of gold here and there, Roy's old pair of charcoal grey winter gloves seemed the obvious choice. A black scarf tied around my nose and mouth did a good job of concealing my facial characteristics, and the only item required to finish off the look was a pair of black sunglasses. Unfortunately the only pair I could find were dark blue, but they were entirely opaque from the outside observer's point of view, and with them placed over my eyes removed the last trace of femininity that would have been discernible to my intended victim.

The next stage was to attempt a dry run while the old pair were not at home, to ensure that when the time came I would be fully equipped to deal with any forced deviations or unexpected surprises, and to ascertain the amount of time needed to leave the flat and get into position, not to mention the best way to escape the scene without being detained or spotted by someone after the attack had taken place. The dress rehearsal went rather well I thought, although the dark sunglasses turned out to be something of a problem. Having turned out the study light and placed them over my eyes I became completely blind and concluded that a pair of ordinary spectacles would have to do as they would at least reflect any light that did hit my face. I knew where to find such a pair of glasses, but having attempted a second run at the full dress rehearsal, and having discovered that my mother's bifocals were almost as much of a hindrance as the blue sunglasses, I conceded defeat and settled for yanking my wooly hat down to my eyelids and pulling my scarf up to almost meet it.

Having never attacked anyone under cover of darkness before, or indeed at any time during daylight hours, I was finding the whole thing, in principle, to be quite exciting and exhilarating. I'd always been fond of detective programmes like Morse and Columbo, and had given great thought over the years to the concept of the perfect crime. In truth I considered no crime to be completely perfect and arrived at the conclusion that it was the inadequacies of the investigator which rendered it insolvable rather than the abilities of the perpetrator. But up until that point in time my contemplation regarding any crime had been entirely hypothetical. It was time to put my theories into practice; to set a date and forge ahead.

A penknife, I concluded, was far too small for the job I had in mind. The old man's eyesight wasn't terribly good and I didn't want to have to wave something about right under his nose for five minutes before he cottoned on to the idea that he was being murdered. A carving knife was the obvious choice, but ours hadn't been sharpened and had a slightly wobbly handle. A baseball bat sprang to mind, but I didn't have one and knew of nobody who played the game, and I doubted that the room available in my chosen spot would be adequate for a full swing. The same was true where a cricket bat was concerned. A tennis racket was too sporty, and a frying pan was far too domestic. We didn't have a chain saw, and although we did have a hedge trimmer, the recharger had melted due to some electrical fault, so it was as dead as a door nail. The only option left open to me was a crowbar. We'd used one to remove the skirting boards when we were decorating, so all I had to do was locate it and I was ready to go. Or at least I should have been.

Given my inexperience when it came to brutally murdering old men, I found myself in need of some final shove in the right direction, as my knees turned to jelly and threatened to withdraw their support. It came on the evening of November 3rd, at about half past nine, about twenty minutes after Roy exited our home to deposit two large black bags of rubbish alongside the hedge at the front of the building. I assumed that he had bumped into a neighbour or paused to fetch something from our car when he did not return immediately, but five minutes became ten, and ten became fifteen, and still he had not returned. Upon reaching the front door I found that the driveway was empty and entirely silent, and Roy was nowhere to be seen. I remained there for a couple of minutes to listen out for Roy's approach, but heard nothing. So, still considering it highly possible that he had been waylaid by a neighbour, but confused by the lack of audible conversation from the street, I put on my coat and made my way to the foot of the steps before pausing again to listen. Upon hearing no sound to indicate Roy's presence or that of anyone else for that matter, I made my way past our car and walked to the front of the drive. I walked onto the pavement and glanced behind the hedge which bordered the property to view the area where the rubbish from our building was left for collection each week, and there, in the road, between the back of the Guppy's car and that of our next door neighbour, I saw my husband lying unconscious on the ground, his shirt smeared with blood.

There was little point in me screaming out for help as nobody within earshot would have lifted a finger to aid either Roy or myself. I made a dash for our front door, picked up the telephone receiver and then replaced it, choosing to grab my handbag and take that with me instead as I returned to the darkened street. Once back by Roy's side, I rummaged around inside the large tapestry covered bag for my mobile telephone and then made the call which brought a squad car and an ambulance speeding towards us less than ten minutes later, by which time Roy was conscious and insistent that I should have called neither. The attending paramedics took little or no time to arrive at the same conclusion Roy had prior to their arrival; that his only serious injury was to the back of his head and, despite the blood stains to the front of his shirt which seemed to suggest otherwise, he had been neither stabbed nor shot. He had received a nasty blow to the head and a punch on the nose, but other than that there was not a mark on him, so despite repeated requests that he reconsider and make the journey to the local hospital to spend the night under observation, Roy was determined that all he really needed was to go back indoors and take a couple of pain killers before going directly to bed.

I was required to make a statement, but considering the fact that I had arrived at the scene after the attack had taken place and hadn't seen a single soul in the street, I could offer no information to assist the police in their inquiries. My suggestion that the Guppys were in some way connected to the assault went down like a lead balloon, and was put down to the ramblings of a distressed and somewhat paranoid wife. The officers insisted that they would try to keep an open mind, suggesting that I do the same until a statement had been taken from my husband, and as Roy was more than willing to speak to the police right away, in spite of the paramedics' insistence that he was not up to the task, the details, or rather the lack of them, were soon revealed to all present.

'I'd seen this guy heading towards me,' Roy began, 'but I didn't think much of it until he spoke. He told me to pay up or else, which made it pretty bloody clear to me that he was another one of the Guppys' henchmen trying to frighten us into giving the nutters what they want. I told him to sod off.'

'And then what happened, sir?' one of the uniforms asked.

'He came at me, and I defended myself.'

The two uniforms inhaled sharply and looked at Roy disapprovingly.

'Someone called out from across the street,' Roy continued, 'and the guy got spooked. I shouted at him to get the hell away from me if he knew what was good for him. Then I heard a noise behind me and realised the bugger wasn't alone... next thing I knew,' Roy raised his hand to the back of his head, 'I felt something hit me, and then I woke up in the road.'

'You say someone called out, sir?' the other uniform inquired.

'Sounded like an old man, but I didn't see anyone.'

'The old man you say you heard,' the first uniform asked. 'You didn't get a look at him then, sir?'

Roy responded in the negative.

'And there was nobody else on the street at the time, sir?'

Roy repeated his response.

'So, nobody else could confirm that the assault took place, sir.' The policeman's words formed a statement rather than a question.

Roy had been right of course. There had been no point in calling the boys in blue. Not only did they express no interest in taking the blooded shirt with them as evidence, suggesting we throw it away as the stain would never come out, but they concluded their visit by indicating that we would only hear from them if the 'mysteriously absent old man' came forward to give a formal statement. The bump of ever increasing proportions on the back of Roy's head, and the paramedics' confirmation that it was highly unlikely to have been self inflicted, went no way in inducing either member of Her Majesty's police force to take the matter seriously. Evidence, as WPC Purser had pointed out so eloquently in the past, was nowhere near as important in a criminal investigation as the solemn word of a fine upstanding member of the local community. The production of the elusive elderly gentleman at the local station, we conjectured, would most likely have inspired no greater interest than Roy's statement had done unless that same gentleman was a member of the Rotary club or a relative of the Mayor.

'I'll be honest with you, sir,' the first uniform explained, despite the fact that his every action suggested he was not capable of being anything of the sort. 'It's unlikely we'll find the two men who you claim attacked you.'

The statement came as no great surprise, as it is imperative that some effort be expended in the apprehension of a criminal, or at the very least that belief in his existence is present, if one is to be caught. So, having been given very little choice in the matter but to take care of the situation ourselves, Roy and I discussed the possibility of contacting another solicitor at length whilst I secretly considered the possibility of my crowbar making contact with Ben Guppy's skull. I was determined to put pay to the old pair's ill deeds once and for all and concluded that a firm date had to be set, so I took out my desk calendar, raised a pin, and struck the paper. 'November 9th it is then,' I thought to myself, as I pencilled in a small cross to mark the spot.

Was I nervous leading up to the evening of the 9th? You'd think I would have been wouldn't you, but I wasn't. Until the moment my plan was put into practise it was entirely theoretical and seemed far removed from my everyday life and quite unreal. I was a character in a book, or on television, and my victim was fundamentally equally fictitious from the point of view that the only place any crime had taken place, up until that point, was inside my head. The preparation was akin to that in the lead up to some amateur dramatic production, and although I did suffer a certain amount of stage fright before my performance commenced, I imagined that was quite natural for a first timer and didn't let it deter me. Roy was presented with a long shopping list at half past eight, told to take his time and have a look at the video selection before returning home, so I was assured of his absence for at least an hour and a half. He was in the car by twenty to nine, after spending five minutes searching for his keys, and was gone only two minutes later. Everything was going perfectly.

I was as cool as a cucumber and quite confident in my abilities right up until the moment I stood in the hallway in full dress, preparing to exit the safety of our home. And then suddenly I wasn't. I can't say that I thought of backing out, as I considered there to be only two possible courses of action at that point, to give in to the old couple or kill one of them, and the former was most definitely not an option. But the fear of being found out, the likelihood that no matter how many unforeseen difficulties had been explored in detail there was bound to be one that had evaded any close scrutiny, and some sudden speculation regarding the unlikely but nonetheless possible existence of a vengeful God and the possibility that he would have something to say about what I was about to do if the day of reckoning came, left me momentarily doubtful and confused, and completely paralysed. There was no qualified coach to cheer me on from the side lines, and despite much research on the Internet it appeared that nobody had seen fit to publish a self help guide for someone planning to murder Ben Guppy. I was entirely alone, and very much aware of the fact.

Having finally plucked up the courage to open the front door and emerge in my transformed state, I got half way down the steps from the flat only to be startled and forced back indoors by the sound of my mobile telephone ringing in my pocket. And when I say ringing, I actually mean to say that it was playing the theme tune to the Lovejoy TV series, and quite loudly too. Once safely inside with the door closed behind me, I discovered that the caller was my mother, so I put down my crowbar, pulled the scarf down from around my mouth and nose, lifted the right side of my wooly hat to enable me to hold the telephone against my ear, and indulged in five minutes of discussion concerning the best way to bake a courgette gratin and the difficulties involved in bathing an ageing and rather wilful Cocker Spaniel.

Having lost time, and a considerable amount of my nerve, I prepared for my second attempt at leaving the flat. It wasn't so difficult the second time around, and I soon found myself half way down the steps again. And then it began to rain. The weather had not been a considered element of my plan. On a dry evening the old man always dropped his wife off and then pulled his car around to the rear of the property to park it inside his garage, so Pat Guppy would go inside and switch off the hall light long before her husband meandered along the drive at a leisurely pace and entered the pitch black area beneath the steps. But occasionally, if the rain was heavy, he would park the car on the street and walk her to their front door under cover of a rather large umbrella. The other unexpected aspect of a rainy night was its effect upon my wooly hat. Having commenced very suddenly, the rain was instantly very heavy and soaked my hat through before I had time to travel the required distance from the foot of the stone steps to the shadows beneath them. Apart from having an unexpectedly cold head, the water which was making its way from the top of my hat and down through its thick fibres eventually found my face and proceeded to cover every exposed area of it before making its way into my eyes.

With vision blurred and shivering from the cold, I positioned myself inside the small cupboard opposite the old couple's front door, and as I stood there, awaiting the Guppys' arrival and holding onto the cold metal shaft of my crowbar, the evening air was filled with the sound of water dripping down from the archway above and the chattering of my teeth.

The old couple were late, and I cursed them for it. But at least the rain had stopped by the time they finally arrived home, and the umbrella had no need to make an appearance. The sound of the small car's engine, as it sat purring on the drive, with headlights full on to light the old woman's way to her front door, filled the cold night air. I listened as the sound of a key entering the lock was followed by that of the thick wooden door creaking shut. The old man shifted gear and pulled away. And then I waited. Overhead a multitude of small fizzing fireworks preceded the loud bangs and sizzles of more elaborate and sizeable showers of coloured light, which were followed in turn by the whizzes and whistles of rockets shooting far off into the night sky. A chorus of crackles and booms ended the display, cloaking the sound of approaching footsteps and leaving me unprepared for the arrival of the old man as he mounted the step and readied himself to go indoors. I had intended to fling open the door and jump out in a show of violent aggression, but the old man had backed away from his portal as he fumbled with his keys and had placed himself close to the cupboard, blocking my exit. My initial attempt to emerge resulted in the thick wooden cupboard door smacking the old man across his back before rebounding against my face. And then, as the late starters exploded in the night sky, casting a green and purple glow over all that stood below, I saw her. As she turned to see what had been the cause of the blow to her back, Pat Guppy came face to face with her assailant, and I was confronted by the second somewhat inconvenient hiccup in my meticulously planned plot to assassinate her husband. She was not he.

Pat Guppy did not scream or call out, but said 'oh' instead as she cocked her head to one side and attempted to recognise me as friend or foe. Had I been her, the crowbar would have been a definite clue, but I was not. She stood motionless for what seemed like an eternity and then, as I raised my crowbar, threw herself backwards against her own front door, cracking her head against it before gradually sliding down it onto her bottom as her legs gave way. And thus we arrived at the moment I had waited for, although admittedly without my intended target. The option of pushing her over had been removed as she had done the job for me, so a blow to the head seemed in order. But as she sat there on the wet ground, whimpering and covering her face with her hands to protect it as she cowered before me, I could do nothing but stare at the pathetic figure at my feet. She was frightened and, very much against my will, I felt pity. I hesitated, and the moment to act had passed. As the light in the Guppys' hallway was switched on, and the old woman slid further down until she was practically sprawled out across the tiles, I fled the scene. I rounded the corner at the bottom of the steps at speed, ascended, paused just long enough to unlock the front door, opened it, slammed it behind me, and headed along the hallway. And then, having managed to reach the bathroom just in time, I fell to my knees and regurgitated the entire contents of my stomach into the toilet.

With the toilet flushed, twice, and the clothes I had worn removed from my body and thrown into the washing machine for a full wash with pre-soak, I donned attire more befitting an ordinary married housewife on a Saturday evening at home, namely a pure white bathrobe and matching head towel to conceal my damp and dishevelled hair, lit several aromatic tea lights which filled the flat with the aroma of freshly baked apple and cinnamon pie, put on some atmospheric music, and awaited the arrival of the police. I had assumed that they would appear within minutes of receiving an emergency call, so despite the likelihood that they would go into the flat below to take a statement before rushing up to arrest me, felt it was safer to allow myself only five minutes at most to affect the transformation from male thug to demure little woman at home. I did it in six, so overshot my own deadline by only sixty seconds, and the rapid response officers still had not arrived by that time.

Fifteen minutes later the boys in blue were still nowhere to be seen, and the driveway was empty and silent, so I considered it possible that the old pair had decided against calling the police. There was arguing below me which was rather audible, but nothing screamed by either party gave me any clue as to their plan of action regarding the events which had just taken place. I sat patiently and awaited some development, and took the time to contemplate my blunders and the possibility of being caught out as a result of them.

After twenty minutes of discussion with the two old dears downstairs, having arrived a full thirty minutes after I had returned indoors, two police officers climbed the steps to our flat and the doorbell rang. After adjusting the collar of my robe to reveal a little more of what lay beneath, and picking up what was left of a cheese and pickle sandwich, I opened the front door, still chewing, and paused for aesthetic effect as I was faced with two middle aged pot-bellied policemen. The younger of the two was immediately taken with my cleavage, whilst the older seemed more interested in my sandwich. There are invariably two things which interest men most when you remove sport from the picture, and they are sex and food, so to be on the safe side I catered for both.

I said nothing. After all, what do you say to two policemen who call at your door at quarter past ten at night? The news is most certainly going to be bad, so you wait and let them be the ones to break the silence. And they did.

'Is your husband at home?' the older of the two officers asked. 'Mr Roy Leah,' he continued, making sure I knew which one of my husbands he was referring to.

'He's out. Can I help?'

The younger of the two policemen stepped forward and gestured towards the hallway behind me. 'Perhaps we could go inside?' he asked, suggesting a choice which he clearly believed didn't actually exist.

I was all too eager to assist and made both men feel very much at home, offering tea and biscuits as they slumped back in the soft armchairs, before asking what had brought them to my doorstep that cold and miserable night.

'Your neighbour, Mrs Guppy, was seriously assaulted earlier this evening,' the older officer said. 'Can you tell us where your husband is?'

The sound of a key in the lock of the front door, followed by Roy calling out that he was home and the sound of carrier bags rustling as he manoeuvred his way along the hallway, alerted the two men to his presence. They both rose from their seats. A short exchange, detailing the events of the evening and the physical state of the old woman, which had apparently deteriorated after three large glasses of brandy, was followed by the voicing of some concern, at the behest of Ben Guppy, that Roy was the one responsible for Pat Guppy's scraped knees and bruised bottom. The accusation was countered by the production of a time stamped shopping receipt, an assurance that Roy's features would have been captured at the local petrol station as he stopped by to fill up, and a full rundown of his movements since leaving home earlier that evening, including a lengthy description of the fifteen minutes he'd spent at the bread counter in Tesco's trying to find someone to slice a large white Bloomer. Having cautioned Roy that every detail would be checked, double checked, and dragged slowly through the wringer to ascertain the level of truth contained within it, the two bobbies informed us that they would be in touch and summarily departed.

In much the same way that misconceptions regarding the inherent goodness of old people facilitate an elderly man's ability to behave criminally and get away with it, misguided beliefs regarding the fairer sex's incapacity for violence afford her a greater level of reverence and respect than her male counterpart. There remains an underlying and deeply rooted romanticised belief, despite claims to the contrary and to the existence of equality between the sexes, that the physically inferior female, especially the domesticated variety, has a predisposition towards kindness, and a natural capacity for goodness. She is free of most of the flaws associated with men, and is wholly unaware of the true evil that exists in the world, having been protected from it by her father and then her husband throughout the entirety of her life, so she is highly unlikely to take any active part in adding to it. Perhaps men foster this belief not to enslave the fairer sex, but simply because the alternative, the acceptance that a woman is just as capable of violence as a man, would shake the very foundations of civilised society and remove any perceived hope for the salvation of mankind, in much the same way as it would if we were to accept that the elderly do not necessarily gain any great wisdom with age and are fundamentally just young people who have lived longer. The only thing which balances the scales when the bad deeds of men are weighed up is the goodness of women and the elderly. And for that reason it did not cross the minds of either of the two policemen, or indeed the Guppys themselves despite being composed of a rotten male and an equally rotten, if not more so, member of the opposite sex, that I might have been the perpetrator of so heinous a crime.

It is the nature of small tightly knit communities filled with small narrow-minded individuals, even if they are in actual fact a part of a larger and more widely populated area, that vicious gossip about one of the locals spreads from one person to another like wild fire, usually in several forms and in both the long and short version, and invariably reaches the ears of those it concerns most, despite not being intended for their consumption, after having made the rounds of every other household. Pat Guppy's version of the events of November 9th was no exception, and after being discussed and speculated upon for only four days, it made its way back to Roy, via James Floyd.

'He threatened me verbally,' had been Pat Guppy's response, when Floyd had had the audacity to question her ability to instantly recognise the man who'd attacked her, as she'd claimed already that he was masked. 'He said he'd slit me open, and I recognised his voice. I was very insistent to the police about that.' She nodded as she spoke, her eyes narrowing as she demonstrated, by much pursing of the lips and sucking of the teeth, the strength of her conviction regarding that one point and her determination, when addressing the boys in blue, to make sure it was heeded and acted upon. 'And in any case, Roy and what's-her-name are the only people in the world who do not like me.'

Floyd indicated that he'd nodded in agreement regarding the final part of the old woman's statement, as he'd felt there was little else he could do despite believing the contrary.

'Those two have never once given me the opportunity to shine you see,' the old woman had concluded when considering the reason for our unwillingness to appreciate her greatness. And in response to Floyd asking how the police had responded to her claims, she replied: 'They said that they will not rest for one moment until Roy Leah is brought to justice. They were most put out that a senior member of the Committee for the Removal of Park Benches was brutally attacked like that. After all, if the chairwoman of Save the Goobrey Amateur Dramatics Association Tea Stall isn't safe, well who is?!'

Pat Guppy was a victim. A crime had been committed and she'd not been the perpetrator, and that in itself had left her disorientated and confused. Never having been the innocent party before, during the days which followed the evening of the 9th the old woman appeared unsure as to what was expected to fulfil the role, and her family and most ardent supporters were equally uncertain and therefore ill equipped to advise her. As news of her brush with death had spread, so too did the rumour that her friends in both high and low places had struck her from their Christmas card list. So, having concluded that some drastic action was necessary to restore her to favour, she spent a few days canvassing the locals, covered from head to foot in the most serious and severe shade of black she could find. A few laps up and down the road, a cup of tea next door, and one across the street, were followed by an offer of assistance to number fifteen, who were in the process of applying for planning permission for an extension to the rear of their semi-detached. She suggested to several, with children who were in need of a job, that the local council had several vacancies and a nod and a wink from her in the right direction would go some way in securing those positions for the deserving young people. And when she spoke to the old chap who lived directly opposite us, who took little interest in local gossip, rarely left his home, and could most likely have passed away without anyone's attention being drawn to his absence for several months, she reminded him that he had been broken into once before when he had refused to assist her, and suggested he should give some serious consideration to that before refusing to sign the petition she would soon be compiling.

We had seen it all before. The canvassing, the threats, the parading and hand shaking, and the waving at passing traffic. The claims of power and influence, which she had never succeeded in proving in any way in her dealings with us, were made to neighbours, passers by, anyone using the post box across the street, and to a door-to-door salesman who called with a selection of face towels and dish cloths.

The routine was a tried and tested one, the vocabulary predictable and uninspiring. The presence of her devoted disciples was expected, as was their willingness to stand around in the drive for hours awaiting our appearance, and their hasty disappearance following it. The loud remarks and fist waving in the direction of our CCTV cameras was rehearsed prior to execution, and there were always a few who forgot their lines or failed to come in on cue. Everything was just as it should have been, with one very distinct alteration. The lady in black herself went to great lengths to avoid being anywhere near Roy or myself, and exited the scene at great speed when either one of us appeared. If she failed to notice the approach of one of us, and escape was quite impossible, she sought refuge in the safety of large numbers and withdrew within the folds of the group. And when forced to enter or leave the property alone, in the absence of any suitable chaperone, she did so at speed and with her head bowed.

For a fortnight following the old woman's ordeal, her husband was surprisingly attentive. Having been accustomed to walking ten paces in front of his wife or an equal number to the rear, throughout their marriage, it must have taken some considerable effort to suppress his dislike for her long enough to accompany her on and off the property as she went about her business. When arriving home after an evening out, the old man would pull up onto the drive and exit their car, and then proceed to investigate the area in front of his front door fully, and quite dramatically, before putting on a light to illuminate a path to their home and allowing the old woman to exit their vehicle. He would take her arm and assist her as she struggled to achieve an upright position, and he would offer support as she limped towards their front door. They would pause, just momentarily, and he would wait patiently as she attempted, often with several false starts, to mount the step in front of their door. Then, having satisfied himself that there was no stranger nearby and no shadow for any large brute to leap from, he would return to his car and drive to the rear of the property before checking every inch of his garage, his garden, and the drive between the two. And this continued each and every evening for around two weeks, after which time Roy commented to me, after observing a change in the ceremony we'd witnessed since the attack, that the old man had returned to dumping his wife out of their car like a sack of potatoes and leaving her to fend for herself in the dark. The old woman's limp disappeared with the old man's staged concern for her, but her unwillingness to be anywhere we happened to be did not.

CHAPTER NINE

BEN Guppy was as fond of Tesco's supermarket as he was of the post office and all its employees. He had a casual relationship with Marks & Spencer, in so much as he stole their carrier bags to make his shopping look more upmarket when his wife had company, but he never did any serious shoplifting anywhere other than Tesco's. His affection for that store was such that he often felt the need to visit it two or three times a day, regardless of any need for a bottle of milk or packet of biscuits, and he was incredibly distressed when he first discovered that we had been shopping at the same location. After spying the largest quantity of Tesco's carrier bags he had ever seen, all brimming with boxes and tins and packets of this or that, making their way up the steps to our flat, his outrage had more than tripled in intensity upon realising that the charming middle-aged man doing the heavy lifting was none other than a member of the Tesco home delivery service team. The old man stood on the drive, fixed firmly to the spot, and shook visibly as two cartons of tangy orange juice in full possession of their orangey bits were offered as replacements for the smooth juice which had been ordered, and then gasped and began to stamp his left foot as the cartons were rejected and had to be returned to the waiting van.

One afternoon, in the middle of December, presumably in need of confirming his darkest fears that we desecrated his sacred territory on a regular basis and were not simply casual shoppers who used the store when Asda was closed, Ben Guppy rushed out of his flat, having heard us descend the external steps from our home and, as we got into our car and prepared to pull out of the drive, ran onto the street and jumped into his own vehicle. As we exited the drive and travelled along the street away from our home, the old man and his shiny red car followed closely behind. He remained in our rear view mirror, grasping his steering wheel and leaning as close as he could to his car's windscreen, as we navigated the roads between our home and the supermarket and, as we arrived at the car park outside the store, he parked in the closest spot to the one we'd chosen and sat observing us as we made our way to the automatic doors. We secured a trolley and opened out our shopping list as we prepared to move amongst the fruit and vegetables, while the old man snatched up a basket and, perhaps fearing that allowing too much of a distance to accumulate between us may result in the subject of his surveillance being lost, began to follow up the rear, allowing no more than three feet to exist between us at any given time.

If we turned around to look at a tin of soup or a packet of cereal, the old man raised his empty basket to cover his face and jumped sideways in an attempt to disguise himself behind a woman two feet shorter than him or a large bag of potatoes. As we filled our trolley and travelled along the aisles, possibly driven by the desire to be perceived as an ordinary shopper with no sinister motive, he began piling any old items into his basket, including a bag of baby nappies and three stainless steel whisks. Whilst I could understand his need for baked beans and a loaf of bread, and imagined he would probably find a use for a tin of Pedigree Chum, despite having no pet dog at home, I couldn't conceive of any reason for him requiring three boxes of Tampax 'super' tampons.

Having reached the checkout, the old man stood closely by and watched as each item was loaded into several of the carrier bags he loved so very much. With wide eyes he monitored the deposit of every tin and packet, and licked his lips as a large fruit cake and a couple of tubs of ice cream travelled towards us on the checkout's conveyor belt. There was a bench nearby, provided for the use of tired customers who required a short rest before lugging their numerous purchases to the vehicles parked outside, so, realising that the tilling up of such a quantity of goods was likely to take more than a couple of minutes, he sat down and made himself more comfortable. Someone had left a newspaper on the seat beside him, and a headline appeared to catch his attention, so he raised the paper and opened it out. Then, having caught up with some of the world's news, he turned the paper over and checked the football results. As Roy offered a credit card in payment for our shopping, and I placed our bags of food into the awaiting trolley, the old man appeared unaware of our imminent departure and, as we moved away from the till and wished the cashier a Merry Christmas, remained seated on his bench, entirely engrossed in the contents of his free broadsheet. I have no idea how long the old man remained there on his bench, or what his reaction was to discovering that we had slipped away unnoticed, but he did not return home until an hour and a half after we were safely indoors, and he looked more than a little confused when he did.

Apparently having acquired a taste for covert surveillance and believing himself more than slightly skilled when it came to tailing either one of us, the old man took to rushing out each time Roy left our flat, walking behind him, or sometimes at his side. Now and then, whilst appearing quite impressed with himself for being so downright clever, he would walk in front of Roy to prevent the neighbours from suspecting him of behaving in an inappropriate manner, and to suggest that Roy was the one doing all the following. But that method brought with it the necessity to turn regularly to ascertain whether or not his subject was still present and, as he'd suffered a sharp pain to the back of his neck twice in the course of doing this and had lost his footing once after failing to realise that he'd reached the end of the pavement whilst engaged in the same occupation, he preferred to remain at the rear when there were few people about to consider his activities suspicious.

After a fortnight of intense scrutiny and continual surveillance I imagine that the old man knew more about my husband's comings and goings than I did. He watched and waited, surveilled and shadowed, and when Roy remained indoors, giving the old man no opportunity to feast his eyes on the subject of his intense fascination, or slink behind him mirroring his every move, he raised his fists to the CCTV cameras and shouted, goaded, and threatened, to release a little of the steam that had built up under his bonnet. And despite the old man's assertions, to all who would give him the time of day, that Roy was plotting to murder Pat Guppy in cold blood, and his seemingly increasing faith in his claim actually being true, old man Guppy thought nothing of tailing the would-be murderer to our garage in pitch darkness, or to any other area of the property for that matter, with little regard for his own personal safety. When considering his actions there is no doubt in my mind that the old man deserved to be killed, even if it were just as a reward for his constantly outstanding display of maliciously motivated stupidity.

The old man's interest in Roy's activities within our garage were not confined to the night time. He was equally curious, in fact maybe even more so, during the daytime. He would rush out of his flat at great speed whenever he saw Roy head along the side of the building towards the rear of the driveway and, as Roy unlocked the garage doors and went inside, the old man would follow suit and enter his own similar structure at high speed and with great excitement. We had often wondered, up until that time, why Ben Guppy chose to position himself inside his garage when the object of his observations was in the building alongside and entirely out of sight. We had supposed that a better view of Roy's activities would be afforded from a position on the driveway or within the old man's garden. But we were wrong. Despite our garage having a window in each door, those small squares of cracked glass had been considered inadequate by the old couple for viewing the internals of their neighbour's outbuilding, and were most certainly too dirty, considering the dismal light conditions of the interior, to provide a clear view all the way to the back wall. So, having found that one of the bricks in the party wall between our garage and the Guppys' was surrounded by crumbling mortar, the old man had dug it out and removed the brick to get a better look. The existence of this peep hole, which allowed a clear view of any activity performed within our garage, became apparent one afternoon when Roy, who had been picking up some tools, spotted light coming from a small gap in the wall opposite him. As he approached the source of the light and bent down to see what the cause was, he was greeted by an empty space where a brick should have been and the sight of the old man's bloodshot eyes looking back at him.

The old man, angered by being found out, leapt back from the wall.

'Bastard!' Ben Guppy shouted, as he flung open one large wooden door and kicked at the other. 'Little bastard!' he screamed at the top of his voice before exiting the building and positioning himself on the driveway. 'Grrrrrrrrrr,' he growled, gnashing his false teeth together.

He slammed the garage door shut and backed away, awaiting the appearance of his enemy, rolling up his sleeves as if preparing for a bout of fisty-cuffs as he strutted back and forth, left and right and yapped like an excited poodle.

'I'll have you!' he called out, looking around to see if anyone in the vicinity had been impressed by his show of masculine prowess. Then, seeing some slight movement, as one of our garage doors inched forward as the wind caught it, and perceiving it to be a sign that Roy would soon appear, he took one giant stride backwards before shooting off down the drive in the direction of his portal.

'You won't be so lucky next time,' he warned just before he crossed the threshold to his home. 'You'll see!' And then the door was slammed firmly shut.

Roy approached the old couple's flat, having taken ten minutes or so to finish what he was doing inside the garage before making his way back along the drive. The Guppys' front door catch went click, click, click. He passed by their front door. Click, click, click, click. He headed towards the stone steps at the side of the building and prepared to make his way to the first floor. Click... click, click. As he reached our home and was about to enter, the old pair's front door was opened and closed, opened and closed, and then opened again one last time before being slammed hard. Then click, click... click.

Whilst the old man continued along the same path he'd travelled since our arrival, although with fewer marbles in his pouch if appearances were not deceiving, the old woman's behaviour was much altered. Unable to muster enough interest amongst the locals to facilitate organising the meeting of even the smallest rowdy mob, she settled for Mrs Palmer from next door and Mr Axley, whose fondness for large women and surgical stockings, he confessed, secured his affection for her for all time. Paranoid in the extreme, although admittedly with some good reason at that point, each little mishap or unexplained event that had some detrimental effect upon the pair was deemed to have been the result of some action on our part, and her two trusted allies were called to come over immediately to lend a shoulder to cry on and an ear to be bleated into. We were blamed for a power outage which left their flat in total darkness for half an hour, despite the fact that every other household in the street suffered the same loss of electricity. The failure of their TV aerial to pick up channel five was also apparently our fault and we were accused of having tampered with it, in spite of the fact that it was located on the roof, forty or so feet above the ground. The misdirection of their mail to the building next door aroused suspicion, as did the delivery of two pints of milk by the milkman as opposed to three. And following the cutting back of each and every tree in the road by the local council, and the subsequent deposit of numerous branches over the walls of neighbouring properties, the discovery of two large ones inside the confines of the old couple's garden, after Ben Guppy arrived home, gave rise to the loud accusation that we had been responsible for the attack on the local greenery, and resulted in the old man beating one of the branches against the front of our garage before hurling it across the drive and issuing a two fingered salute in the direction of our kitchen window.

Pat Guppy remained out of sight while her husband was consistently in plain view. Unable to muster the courage to occupy her previous observational position outside her front door whenever we went out or returned home, which caused her some very obvious annoyance, the old woman made her presence felt by switching the lights in the old couple's bedroom on and off repeatedly whenever we came into sight. The flashing of the light bulbs in the old couple's flat, as they moved around their home and increased their electrically illuminating activities from just one room to any one of four, depending on which area of the drive we'd been spotted in, was often accompanied by that of the flash of the old man's camera, and it was not entirely unusual to find Pat Guppy manning the light switch in one room while her male accomplice carried out similar duties in the room alongside the one occupied by his wife. On, off. On, off. And then a total blackout as the old pair observed our reaction to their efforts.

The Guppys were used to being noticed. They were used to being listened to. They were used to being feared. Having spent years building a reputation, and feeling that they had achieved a position of power within the community which many envied, the old pair had worked incredibly hard since our arrival to maintain the high level of respect they had assumed existed previously. They cared more for the protection of that investment than they did for the acquisition of wealth, which was certainly saying something because little inspired them to act more than the sight of a ten pound note. But having noticed some considerable decrease in the local populace's reverence for them, the old pair became visibly desperate, then annoyed, and finally vengeful. In truth, there had been no decrease in admiration, respect, or adulation. Those things would have had to exist in the first place for there to be any subsequent reduction in them. The dislike and indifference, and in some cases sheer hatred, that locals felt towards the Guppys had been thinly concealed behind an outward display of obedient respect for many years. The true nature of their feelings had, however, always been discernible to those who did not possess the old couple's amazing propensity for arrogant stupidity.

Having been robbed of the rights and entitlements which the old couple knew instinctively were theirs by merit of having passed the age of sixty, they sought to take them back, and to see that we paid for having stolen them in the first place. The idea that an individual should earn respect was an entirely unfamiliar concept to the old pair, and any suggestion that it applied to those of advancing years would have had the old lady spitting chips and clutching at her chest as her heart failed due to shock. Feeling that some show of power was necessary if they were ever to regain their standing in the local community, and perceiving some need to act quickly as they were due to visit their son-in-law for Christmas, Ben Guppy exited his flat during the morning before Christmas Eve and positioned himself in his car, which was parked alongside the exit to the drive and almost entirely concealed from our view by the hedge of our neighbour, and awaited the emergence of Roy or myself. He was there for some time, with his window wound down, audibly cursing our existence and our fondness for staying in bed late, but at midday, as we left our home and prepared to make a journey into town to do some last minute Christmas shopping, his patience was rewarded. We got into our car and proceeded to reverse slowly out of the drive and onto the empty street, while the old man climbed out of his vehicle and approached at speed. Having produced a large and rusted paint tin, he advanced towards the window on Roy's side of our car and took a thick brush from the pocket in his jacket, before dipping it into the tin, and daubing a large quantity of what was once pure brilliant white emulsion paint across the glass before him. Realising that the door on the driver's side was already partly open by the time he had finished what he'd set out to do, the old man, having anticipated some delay on our part which would have comfortably accommodated his escape, flung what remained of the white paint, in its dented tin, over the top of our car and onto the edge of our garden, and then ran like the wind along the driveway in the direction of his front door, calling out to his wife to open up as he approached safety. The door was slammed shut.

'Let me in!' the old man screamed. 'For God's sake woman, what are you playing at?'

Bang, bang, bang. He hammered his fists against the painted surface of the heavy wooden door. Clack, clack, clack. He began tapping the knocker against it's brass plate.

'Pat! Let me in!'

The door remained shut. The old man continued beating it. Roy and I sat silently within our car observing the scene.

'Paaaaaaaaaaat!' He leapt into the air as he screamed, kicking at the door and waving his arms about above his head. 'Pleeeeeeease!'

A small group of school children gathered nearby the stone gatepost and giggled. A young woman approached with a pushchair and beckoned to her friend to come and see the funny old man jumping about like a monkey at the zoo. A couple out walking their dog paused to see what the fuss was all about. Curtains twitched. Neighbours looked on. And tongues began to wag.

Emulsion paint is water soluble; something Ben Guppy overlooked when he emptied a large dollop of it onto our car. While the old man hopped and skipped about the drive, still trying to figure out a way to entice his wife to compromise her own safety by permitting him access to his home, Roy attached a hose pipe to a nearby outdoor tap and washed away the chalky white puddle of paint.

'Did he do this?' one of the throng of observers inquired, gesturing towards the old man.

'Yes, I saw him,' came the response from a second.

At the suggestion from another that the police should be called, as a witness was present and the old man was clearly out of his mind, the second speaker disappeared from view and was gone. At the suggestion that the remainder present could at the very least attest to the old fool's insanity, the group dispersed. And at the suggestion that Roy had every right to give Ben Guppy a good hiding, the old man took to his heels, rounded the corner at the end of the drive, and headed up the hill towards the local woods, presumably to find somewhere to hide amongst the overgrown undergrowth.

Later that day, as Roy and I sat down to dinner and Ben Guppy returned to the building under cover of darkness, having relocated his manhood, an argument ensued on the driveway as

Pat Guppy, who claimed to have been worried half to death, accosted her husband on the drive with a dishcloth.

'How dare you go off like that and leave me here with them,' she protested. 'I was terrified!'

'*You* were terrified?' the old man replied. '*I* was the one stuck out here with the bastard just inches from me, waiting to strike.'

'Well, if you were a man...'

'Shut your mouth!' Ben Guppy screamed. 'I've told you, I'll sort it out!'

Pat Guppy raised the dishcloth above her head and brought it down in an arc, flicking it as it made contact with the side of her husband's face. Slap. The old man staggered backwards.

'What was that for?' he demanded.

'You're a failure, a coward and a failure. You've never been any good you stupid old fool.'

'I'll sort it out!' he repeated.

'You've been saying that for fifty-odd years, and I gave up believing you, you... you liar, more than forty ago!' She raised the dishcloth a second time and prepared to strike. The old man dodged sideways and avoided being struck as the cold wet cotton whooshed past his left ear, but walked straight into the follow up attack and received a slap to his right cheek and then one to his forehead.

'Do that again and you'll be sorry,' he warned.

'I'll be *sorry*? I've been sorry since the day I married you, you prat!'

As a young man passed by our garden wall and paused to allow his Labrador a few moments to empty its bladder, the old man caught sight of him and, seeing a smile creep across the observer's face, failed to see his wife coming for a final assault. The wet cloth, spread wide to engulf its target, landed on top of his head and covered his glasses. The young man tried to smother a giggle and failed.

'What are you laughing at?' Ben Guppy demanded repeatedly, as a vast spectrum of colours travelled across his face, beginning with a deep magenta and ending in a dramatically violent shade of purple. 'What's so funny?' he screamed, peeling the dishcloth away from his balding head before tossing it across the drive in the direction of the young stranger. 'I'll kill you, you bastard!' he yelled. 'I swear I'll kill you!'

'You're making a fool of yourself,' Pat Guppy said, as she made her way towards her home. 'As usual.'

'I'll kill you too!' he screamed. Waving his fist and stamping his feet. 'I'll kill all of you!'

CHAPTER TEN

BEN Guppy was annoyed at his inability to convince the general population that he should be taken seriously, and by the end of March seemed to have decided to invest all of his efforts into affecting some change in that area. He engaged in various serious activities, and maintained what he considered to be the fiercest of facial expressions throughout. His wife invited fellow members of this committee or that to their home so that the old man could be seen accompanying them along the drive, which was presumably intended to demonstrate the faith of others in his ability to locate his own front door. He coated his hair with a thick film of oil and combed it in such a fashion that not one carefully positioned strand of it was free to move when urged to do so by the wind, and he maintained a level of shine to the top of his head that was matched only by that present on the bonnet of his car. His shirt collars were stiff, and his trousers were pressed. And when he did venture to sit in his garden with a newspaper and hot beverage, his chosen reading matter was The Financial Times, and his tea was served in his wife's best china teacup. Unfortunately the cost of purchasing that particular newspaper was prohibitive and resulted in him displaying the same edition for days on end when parading the drive, and the breakage of his wife's best cup brought him a cuff to his ear, a blow to his dignity, and a return to the use of a cheap mug. But he persevered nonetheless, and went to every length to avoid being humorous when speaking to neighbours, despite feeling that this deprived them unjustly of a pleasure they had so evidently enjoyed during previous years.

Having popped out to our garage for just a moment, at around half past nine in the evening during the last week in April, Roy was returning to our flat when the old couple's car pulled onto the drive. As he made his way along the rear of the drive, still out of sight of either of the old pair, Pat Guppy opened the passenger door of the shiny red car and began to climb out of her seat. She had one foot firmly positioned on the cold tarmac and had begun to stand when her husband spotted Roy turning the corner at the back of the building as he began his approach towards them. As Pat Guppy shifted her weight onto the leg positioned outside the old couple's car, her husband, suddenly consumed by rage, hit the horn and revved the engine in an attempt to cause his enemy to stand aside or withdraw. Seeing that Roy had continued along the drive, he leaned closer to the windscreen and began hitting it with his open palm, and then, in spite of his wife's position, with one half of her body outside of the vehicle whilst the other half remained inside it, he hit his accelerator and pulled forward in the direction of the object of his immense frustration and annoyance.

'Yeeeeeeeeeeaaaaaaaa!' he screamed as the car jerked forwards.

The old woman's cries did nothing to dissuade the old man from continuing along his chosen course. He was determined to accomplish what he had set out to do, and as the old woman relinquished any remaining hold she had maintained on the car door, and was tossed unceremoniously onto the drive and subsequently onto the bare soil of our garden alongside it, Ben Guppy continued his approach towards Roy, screaming and hitting the steering wheel with his fist. As Roy sprinted to safety, and the old man's shiny red run-around ran out of driveway, the sound of gears crunching and the accelerator screaming filled the air and drowned out the yelps issued from the old woman, who was sprawled across the ground beneath our lilac tree with her skirt hitched up around her bottom.

Under normal circumstances I would have been incredibly put out at the thought of either one of the old pair setting one foot onto our garden, and the attention they had paid it in the past had caused both Roy and myself a great deal of annoyance, but considering the circumstances of that evening I didn't much mind the old woman's continued presence upon our soil, and was more than willing to grant her an extended stay. The old man, having leaned across and closed the passenger door for fear that it would be damaged otherwise, had continued his attempts to manoeuvre in the drive, in spite of Roy's exit from it, and seemed unhurried in his desire to remove the old woman from her prostrate position on our land. Having finally given up on the idea of running Roy down, he paused momentarily and appeared confused as to the location of his wife. He exited his vehicle and walked a little way along the drive, looking this way and that before spotting her lying on the ground, opposite his front door. Then, after walking to the rear of the drive and unlocking the padlock which kept the large mouldy wooden doors of his garage firmly closed, he returned to his car before parking it up for the night. Only then did he return to the site of his wife's sudden expulsion from their vehicle, and after a few moments spent ascertaining whether or not she could get up under her own steam and remove the need for him to do his back an injury trying to heave her to her feet, he appeared to accept that she was unconscious, and not just trying it on, and walked slowly into his home to telephone an ambulance.

Pat Guppy's dramatic removal from the premises by paramedics, which had been preceded by the arrival of an ambulance with its bright flashing lights and loud siren, attracted a considerable amount of attention from those living nearby. Conjecture regarding the nature of her injuries, and the likelihood that she would not reach the hospital alive, was rife and quite audible, and several onlookers called out to their family members to telephone this friend or that, as they would not, apparently, have wanted to be deprived of witnessing the old woman's dying moments. Several flashes from the crowd which had congregated at the end of the drive highlighted the presence of a number of amateur photographers, although I doubted that the dim light would have allowed the production of a half way decent image. And the men sent out to offer medical aid were hindered numerous times by requests from those present that they be allowed to see the body. However large an audience she might have expected when she stood to speak at length at some committee meeting or other, Pat Guppy had achieved three times that number for lying flat on her back and saying absolutely nothing at all.

I cannot tell you the extent of the old woman's injuries, as I had little interest in them beyond the hope that they had been fatal. But the rumours which permeated every conversation that took place in the local vicinity over the next couple of weeks had her dead, miraculously unharmed, paralysed, and occasionally decapitated. And conjecture regarding the source of her injuries was equally varied, although a frenzied attack by my husband seemed to be the most favoured explanation for the old woman's demise, and the one most frequently supported by her husband. She remained in hospital for two months, and for the first few weeks of her absence the old man was treated to visits from a steady flow of unattached elderly ladies who were more than willing to tend to his needs with regards to his nourishment, the provision of clean clothes, and any other service that a woman is capable of rendering, in the belief, much encouraged by the old man himself, that his wife would be unlikely to survive much beyond the end of the month, and that he was due a small windfall, in the form of an insurance pay out, in the event of her death.

There was a great deal of interest in the old woman's accident amongst those who lived nearby, and the immense amount of curiosity shown by neighbours was matched only by the apparent lack of concern shown by the old woman's actual family. A steady flow of well wishers with cards, and of old ladies with casseroles, made its way along the drive at all hours of the day following the departure of Pat Guppy. Those who visited would not leave without first uncovering every last gruesome detail of the old woman's accident, and feeling unable to accurately convey the true extent of his wife's injuries by the use of verbal description alone, and in light of the unwillingness of all who called to ascertain the facts from the woman herself via a visit to her hospital bed, the old man returned home from the hospital one evening with a handful of Polaroid photographs of various parts of his wife's anatomy, and proceeded to display them for all interested parties, and to offer, for a small fee, to make photocopies so the images could be taken away and enjoyed at home. But of course the locals' interest waned, as it did with all incidents which were more than forty-eight hours old, and Ben Guppy's fifteen minutes in the spotlight were unceremoniously brought to an end by the sudden announcement by Mr Waters from number forty, who was eighty if he was a day, that his wife, who was several decades his junior, was expecting a baby. The old ladies with baked goods continued arriving below, but the well wishers with cards were relocated to a few doors away, amid much discussion regarding the benefits of taking Viagra and of quitting smoking before the age of forty.

And so, Ben Guppy was left alone. It was an eventuality we had thought desirable up until that point. Knowing that the old woman was the one who had been the brains, for want of a better word, behind most of the old pair's hairbrain schemes, we were convinced that, without her continuing guidance, the old man would lose all sense of direction and that his motivation for continuing the conflict would lessen. Following her sudden removal from the property the old man did appear to flounder at first, but the foundations for each plan contrived by the Guppys had been set in place so long ago, and the routine was so familiar to the old man, that the removal of his wife at so late a stage in the game served only to free him from the constraints on his behaviour which had been maintained by his wife. He continued staring and following, shouting and threatening, photographing and pacing, but he did so to an even greater degree than he had done previously, in the absence of any instruction to stop.

With no wife at home to brow beat him upon his return, the old man took to the bottle and spent his evenings propping up the bar of a local public house. In absolute control of the old couple's finances, he filled his pockets with cash and then emptied them at the local off licence, and empty whiskey bottles began to line up along the wall by his front door as the days passed, having grown in number to such an extent that his dustbin could no longer offer satisfactory accommodation. Often accompanied by one or more members of his harem, and when I say accompanied I mean held up, he would return home intoxicated, and having proved too great a weight for his elderly companions to keep upright would often end his evening sitting on top of our garden soil, propped up against a tree. The elderly ladies were frequent visitors. In actual fact they always had been. But they had come and gone, prior to Pat Guppy's hospitalisation, during the morning while the old woman was out performing her charitable works upon those who were too ill or too old to run away, or between the hours of half past seven and nine o'clock in the evening, when Ben Guppy would return home from dropping his wife off at some function for social climbers who had started at the bottom and were working their way down. The elderly ladies, unlike Pat Guppy, did not seem at all bothered by the old man's continually inebriated state, and often joined in the excessive imbibing, to such an extent that they were frequently compelled, albeit with the aid of a companion to prop them up, or after taking a seat on the steps which led up to our flat, to remove their stockings and wave them above their heads as they headed off home in the dead of night.

Ben Guppy, having run out of space along the wall by his front door, began depositing his empties at the foot of our steps and along our garden border. And whilst drunk, on power as much as cheap whiskey, he would throw them across the drive, and occasionally hurl one at Roy or myself as we made our way home; although possessed of an amazingly bad aim, the projected glass missiles usually missed our heads by a couple of feet and made their way into the front garden of our neighbour, whilst the effort required to launch each bottle saw the old fool falling backwards onto his bottom, often in the direction of a nearby holly bush. He paced the drive, or rather he attempted to, as he often got only a few feet before toppling over, and he sang at the top of his voice at two o'clock in the morning. And amazingly, when you consider that none of the residents of neighbouring properties could have failed to hear his much altered and extremely audible operatic rendition of 'My Old Man's a Dustman' accompanied by himself on percussion, in the form of a stick and a dustbin lid, not one policeman called to quieten him down regardless of the hour of the night or the volume of his singing.

Perhaps wanting to fill the time which had previously been occupied by the cleaning and cooking he carried out under the direction of his wife, the old man sought new pastimes and diversions. He developed an interest in local wildlife, in so much as he took to chasing sparrows across our garden, kicking up the soil as he went. But such pursuits seemed to inspire little long term enjoyment and, possibly motivated by the sudden discovery that his bank account had been drained of funds by his constant draining of bottles from the off licence, he must have decided to open his own business in the form of a car wash, as he emerged from his flat one afternoon with a bucket of dirty water and proceeded to empty the contents onto the bonnet of our car before flinging a dirty wet rag at our bedroom window.

As the weather got warmer and the days longer, the old man's attentions turned to leisure pursuits, and specifically to fishing. One warm Sunday afternoon, with a six pack of Heineken and a small Tupperware tub which contained a handful of garden worms, the old man climbed up onto our garden wall and rolled up the bottoms of his trousers to reveal two skinny white legs and a pair of gartered odd socks. He produced a long garden cane with a lengthy piece of garden string tied to one end of it and, after trying to attach one of the unfortunate garden worms to the hook, which appeared to be fashioned from a paperclip, flung out the cane before winding the line back in by means of an invisible reel, in an attempt to catch himself a nearby magnolia bush.

In the days which followed, the old man's confidence in his own invincibility seemed to experience some resurgence. Possibly spurred on by his intoxicated state, the absence of his wife's criticisms, and the attentions of his admiring elderly ladies, who appeared to have been joined by Mrs Palmer from next door, Ben Guppy returned to openly demonstrating his annoyance at the existence of the CCTV cameras, whilst at the same time appearing wholly unaffected by the purpose they served. With no regard for the fact that his every move was being documented, he shouted at them, he threw stones at them, he threatened to shoot them, and one evening, with the aid of a small ladder and an old wooden mallet, he climbed the wall at the side of the property, reached up, and began beating the bricks violently in an attempt to smash one of the cameras to pieces, despite it still being more than five feet out of reach. He continued pacing the drive throughout the day, pausing every so often to smile and pull out his tongue at anything that moved, or didn't as the case may be, before rushing about furiously, screaming at the top of his voice that he would make us pay for what we had done to him, and then making a dash to the front of the drive before kicking our car's tyres and spitting at the bonnet. At night he would walk back and forth, watching the sensor lights triggering and attempting to ascertain whether or not the system could monitor his every movement after dark, and he would stand below our bedroom window, sometimes for an hour or more, or climb onto the bonnet of our car and sit there mouthing threats and waving his arms.

The old man's numerous empty bottles remained outside his front door, although their number did not increase. But despite having no further occasion to see him in the presence of a full can of beer, a bottle of whiskey, or any other alcoholic beverage for that matter over the following days, the drunken behaviour continued nonetheless. He still wandered this way and that, but the falling over was far less frequent, and despite continuing his late night warblings he appeared to have learned the words to each of his chosen songs and was considerably more adept at remaining in key. The visits by his harem decreased dramatically and eventually stopped altogether, and in the absence of any assistance when returning home from the pub the old man seldom managed to reach the soft soil of our garden before collapsing, more often than not being forced to spend the night spread out on the drive behind out car. And when he did manage to reach his own front door, he seldom possessed the dexterity required to unlock it, so wound up sleeping on his doorstep, or attempting to travel the remaining distance to the end of the drive in order to reach the awaiting garden bench.

After six weeks of absence, Pat Guppy's existence appeared to have been entirely forgotten by her husband, who had long since ceased exiting the building each afternoon to make the short journey to the hospital. And to a great extent those who had claimed some close acquaintance with her appeared to have become accustomed to life without her also.

Rumours began to circulate regarding the possibility that she would go straight from the hospital to a nursing home when she was released, although these enjoyed a relatively short life span and were quickly replaced by those which claimed her actual death. So sure were those who facilitated the spreading of that particular piece of speculation that the well wishers who had visited in their droves just following Pat Guppy's initial departure began revisiting the scene of their earlier declarations of hope for her speedy return to health with ones of hope for the old man's eventual recovery from his loss, and his subsequent remarriage as his wife would not, according to them, have wanted him to spend the remainder of his days alone. So touched was the old man by their declarations of sorrow and their offerings of numerous telephone numbers which belonged to this maiden aunt or that widowed mother or sister, that he was almost induced to put on a black arm band and instruct the hospital to ship his wife off to Twilight Years retirement home, until reminded of the cost of residency at such an establishment. He declined one neighbour's offer of a cut price wreath from her sister-in-law who knew the chap who ran the local florist, but made a note of suggested hymns for his wife's funeral, which he passed out for his neighbours' consideration, as he thought they may be of use at a later date.

Any speculation regarding the old woman's passing to the other side was finally put to rest by the appearance of a letter to the editor which was published in the local newspaper during the last week in June. The letter commented on the state of trees in the local area, the need for more leaves on all of them, and the suggestion that squirrels, which were apparently responsible for damage to motor vehicles parked adjacent to a local park, should be castrated in an attempt to slow population growth, and it was signed 'Pat Guppy.' The publication of that single piece of correspondence was intended, in its capacity as an indication of her continuing presence on earth, to be a warning shot across the bow of anyone who had sought to replace her in her absence, whether in her role as wife or local celebrity. It resulted in much chatter amongst the neighbours regarding the old man's lady friends and the appointment of Mrs Palmer, in the old woman's place, as chair of a committee set up to secure the preservation, at much cost to the tax payer, of a local relic which was even more advanced in age than Pat Guppy herself, and was accompanied by a great deal of running about by the old man, who had received the news, according to James Floyd, that his wife's return to his care was imminent. Accustomed to her absence, and fearful of the consequences of her return, the local population retreated behind closed front doors. The whiskey bottles were cleared away, shirt collars were washed, Mrs Palmer went away on holiday, and squirrels across the county shook on their branches at the prospect of the old woman's departure from hospital. It appeared that not one living soul's spirits were raised by the news of her recovery. But while I cannot say that I welcomed the old woman's return to the building as such, I must confess that I did welcome the old man's expected return to sobriety.

And so Pat Guppy made an appearance at the property for the first time in two months, after being deposited on the drive from the rear of an ambulance. She stood motionless for a while, grasping onto the handles of two walking sticks she'd been provided with for support, and surveyed the empty drive before her. The nearby street was empty, not a single person was in sight, and even the passing of nearby traffic seemed to take place in silence. The old man took her arm and attempted to force some movement in the direction of their front door, but she shook off his grip and continued to await whatever it was she had expected, with an expression of ever increasing confusion and annoyance. It seemed that, having witnessed such a large turnout during the evening of her accident, and perceiving such great numbers of onlookers as a demonstration of the fondness she had always assumed existed amongst the locals for one of her importance, she had anticipated a similarly substantial congregation to have formed in anticipation of her return home.

There was no red carpet to soften her approach to her front door, no orderly line of council members and journalists to demonstrate her connections to those in power and subsequently report them to the common man, and no flower girl standing by with a mixed bouquet of pink and peach roses, yellow carnations, and white chrysanthemums. The approach of Mrs Ferris from number thirty-four, who had dropped off the list of chosen people entirely a few months previously after being accused, by Mrs Palmer, of saying hello to me one cold afternoon as I emptied the car of shopping, induced Pat Guppy to speak. 'Piss off' were the words issued in the demoted one's direction. 'Go on, bugger off you old cow!'

She was not the same woman. Despite having the same sour features, malicious twisted soul, an overwhelming desire that everyone around her should suffer, and a strong determination to see that she played some part in bringing that about, she had lost something during those two months away. I'm inclined to suggest it was her marbles. She spent most of her time indoors during the month following her release, but we did see her every now and then, as she made her way out onto the drive with the intention of reminding the neighbours that she still wasn't dead. 'Bugger off, you dirty whore' was her favourite greeting when she saw me outdoors. 'Come here you sick bastard' usually indicated that she wanted to have a quiet word with Roy when he was unfortunate enough to bump into her on the drive.

'Your tree's sick' she would call out, as Roy continued indoors, 'I say, look here, your tree's sick.' And she would repeat it over and over again until he was out of sight. She spent a great deal of her time outdoors examining our lilac tree, and occasionally sent for the old man to come and take a photograph of it. She touched it, pulled at it, stared at it, spoke to it, and eventually began inviting people over to join her as she assessed its condition and compiled an in depth report which she claimed she had been asked to produce for the local council. She directed the same degree of analytical investigation towards our drains and downpipe over the following weeks, and asserted loudly, usually prior to remarks regarding the state of our garden, that the sound of water gushing down the waste pipe from our toilet kept her awake at night. She insisted that she could hear us turn on the taps in our kitchen and bathroom, questioned the need to take a bath everyday when the sound of the tub being emptied caused our neighbours so much distress, and the mere sight of a hose pipe had her almost toppling over as she raised one of the sticks allocated to assist her upright position and attempted to wave it about to indicate the strength of her feeling.

The old woman's obsession with our usage of water grew as the days passed, and we were rarely granted the privilege of flushing the lavatory without the event being followed by several thuds to the ceiling below us and the issuing of an all-points bulletin, the following day, to our neighbours and whoever happened to deliver the old woman's mail or milk. Any attempt to clean our steps was accompanied by much pacing, staring, and picture taking by the old man, with very particular attention being paid to the amount of water left on the ground following such activity. And if Roy dared hose down the drive the old woman would appear in tears, calling out to him to stop because he was making the ground wet. The ridiculous nature of her accusation seemed not to have dawned upon her, and appeared for that matter to have been considered wholly justifiable not just by the old couple themselves but by the few supporters they had managed to hold onto. The mere appearance of either one of us and a watering can brought Mrs Palmer rushing over from next door to give Pat Guppy a hug, and small huddles of affronted and overly excited pensioners began to congregate each time Roy washed down the bonnet of our car, with the intention of witnessing his bad behaviour and testifying to it if the need arose.

CHAPTER ELEVEN

THERE could be only one Benjamin Arnold Guppy. I was so completely convinced that the old man was entirely unique that when my mother said she'd seen another just like him I doubted the accuracy of her statement and told her she needed a new pair of glasses. After all, Mother Nature, I protested, could not be so sadistically unkind as to inflict another so visually and morally hideous upon mankind. And as it turned out, she was not.

My mother had moved to a flat just a few miles from where Roy and I lived not long before we moved into ours. She was instantly aware that one of her neighbours, an elderly woman by the name of Floss Littleworth, was a bit difficult to say the least, but had thought little of it at first as she initially saw very little of her. But as our problems with the Guppys had begun to escalate, her own situation had appeared to develop in tandem, and we had often commented that the three old kooks would get along famously if they were ever to meet as they shared similar character traits and a similarly peculiar obsession with dustbins. It had not been immediately apparent that the events which were unfolding within my mother's building were in any way linked to the incidents taking place in the vicinity of our home, although we had sometimes supposed that the two old women might know each other from some church group or committee.

Floss Littleworth was a small woman. She was not what you would call attractive, unless boney, toothy, and cross-eyed are your cup of tea. Add to that a balding patch on top of her head, ugly footwear, and the fact that she smelled like tripe and onions, and you have a pretty fair idea as to why her husband ran off with a younger model when the old woman's money ran out, and she spent the remainder of her years without male company, or that of any other soul for the most part. People didn't simply cross the road to avoid her, they moved house. Not only was she a very painful sight for sore eyes, she was the nosiest and most malicious little creature you could wish to meet. She journeyed through life leaving those who had the misfortune to cross her path in a state of sheer misery, but she did it with a smile. Heaven forbid that she should raise her voice, she abhorred bad language, and always wiped her feet on the way in. And she was a proud churchgoer. She had trouble with the ten commandments, loving thy neighbour, doing unto others, and all that jazz, but shook the vicar's hand every Sunday morning and was therefore a devout Christian and sure of her eventual place in heaven. She loved God, she told everyone so. Well, it was not difficult to love him, as he was almost as great as she was and never answered her back. It was mankind she had a problem with. People had an annoying habit of refusing to turn around and crouch slightly so she could reach up and drive a sharp blade into their back.

Floss Littleworth was as intrigued by my mother's mail as Ben Guppy was by ours. But whereas our letters and parcels came directly to our own front door and the old man, despite trying repeatedly over the years, had failed to prevent the postman from delivering them directly into our hands for the most part, my mother's mail was posted through a letterbox into a shared hallway before being sorted by whoever happened to reach the communal front door first. And as Floss Littleworth stood sentry from half past seven in the morning, even though the postal delivery never took place until well past nine o'clock, she was always the one who picked up the mail, sorted it into groups, and then took her own mail and some of my mother's before returning to her flat. She would agree to take in any parcel that did not require a signature, and that package and its contents would never be seen again. And when my mother purchased her own private letterbox and fixed it to her garden fence, and instructed the postman to deliver her mail directly to that location from then on, Floss Littleworth, unable to scream her head off as she was known for not losing her temper and cared a great deal for her reputation, picked up the thing nearest to her in the communal hallway, which just happened to be a telephone directory, and launched it at my mother's front door.

Ben Guppy cared a great deal for the contents of the garbage bags we put out for collection every Monday evening. He was happy to stand outside in all weathers and at all hours, looking through our papers and wrappers, packets and tins, picking out the choicest bits. But Floss Littleworth was not the type to spend her time outside up to her elbows in somebody else's garbage. No indeed. She did her sifting indoors. And to that end she emerged from her flat's back door one evening, picked up my mother's dustbin, and made off with it into her own home. She returned it after she was done, but not before removing anything resembling a bank statement or utility bill, and she was particularly fond of discarded greeting cards or private letters. And in the weeks that followed, having been told that my mother and sister were both vegetarians, Floss Littleworth lined the bottom of my mother's dustbin, immediately after it had been emptied by the refuse collectors, with chicken bones and the bits that had been left over from her Sunday roast, or the odd part-nibbled pork chop.

Having been deprived of the ability to pilfer mail and, with the relocation of the dustbin to a locked shed, the ability to sift through garbage to glean titbits of information about my mother and sister, Floss Littleworth got herself into quite a state. She found that tossing books and door mats around the communal hallway brought little relief, and left her open to ridicule from anyone who caught her in the act, and my mother's unwillingness to enter into any dialogue with her by that point left her unable to voice her feelings and vent her frustration. So, feeling that some demonstration of her distress was called for, in the hope that it would negatively impact upon my mother's ability to enjoy living in her home, the old woman exited her flat and made her way to the fence which stood in the courtyard directly opposite my mother's kitchen window. She placed a basket of washing onto the ground, and then began emptying its contents, one item at a time. Each garment turned out to be an item of underwear, still dripping wet from the washing machine, and shortly after being picked out from the pile, a pair of knickers or a brassiere was attached, by means of the nails which already existed along the wooden panels, or by the addition of drawing pins, along the length of the fence. The view from the kitchen window had never been anything to write home about, and my mother had often commented that the fence she was forced to stare at each time she visited the sink to do the washing up was much in need of a coat of paint or varnish to liven up its appearance, but she longed for those bare, battered and decidedly grey lengths of weathered wood in the days that followed, as another pair of stockings or a well worn brassiere was added to the display.

There was no motor car for Floss Littleworth to chase, so she ran after my mother's bicycle instead. Having been prevented from digging up my mother's garden by the erection of a tall wooden fence along the boundary, and a locked gate, she made do with leaning over the lowest section to steal potted plants. And while Pat Guppy was standing on the corner of the two roads which passed in front of and alongside our home, gathering support from those who lived nearby in her quest to see us ruined, Floss Littleworth was knocking on the doors of each of her neighbours with tales of the wild parties my mother had been having, the bags of empty booze bottles that were put out with the rubbish each week, and the strange men who came and went at all hours. She stared from behind net curtains, she stared through windows into homes that were not her own, she pointed, she lied and defamed, and she followed my mother and sister about the place, monitoring their every move. And then one day she received a visitor in a shiny red car, and all the pieces of the puzzle began to fall into place.

Having been formally introduced to Ben Guppy only once, almost three years earlier, and having seen very little of him since then, my mother could not claim to have total recall with regards to the old man's facial features or physical stature. He was an unremarkable old man in many respects, despite his remarkably unattractive appearance, so he had not left any deep impression upon her memory. But she telephoned me one afternoon in August to ask if I knew whether or not the Guppys had any relatives in the area. She couldn't be sure, she said, but she could have sworn that she'd just seen a man who could very well pass for Ben Guppy's brother on the street in front of her flat. And it had not been the first time. She'd caught a glimpse of the man several times previously when he had been hanging around in the road nearby, but he'd been so far away or had passed in front of her so briefly that she could not be certain before then that he did resemble the old man so closely. But he'd stood right in front of her for a minute or so that day, and the resemblance was so striking that she'd called my sister, Stella, to come and have a look at him, and they'd been in agreement that he was just as physically repulsive as Ben Guppy and, if anything, was more unattractive, despite appearing to have more hair. She had concluded that the old man had a twin or perhaps a doppelganger.

Two Ben Guppys. The mere notion made my skin crawl. It occurred to me that there could be others out there who afflicted an equal amount of pain upon the eyes, but it seemed unlikely that two would be created in the same town. That much ugliness, both visual and internal, I assumed, would be spread out across the globe and could not occur in a cluster in one location as it would upset the natural balance of things. Although, I supposed that if it were possible for all the beautiful people to be born in California it would be equally possible that all the ugly ones had been let loose on the west coast of England.

Then the little red car had pulled up, and Floss Littleworth's visitor had emerged, holding a bunch of wilting carnations. He had dressed up, and was wearing a clean purple shirt, or at least one where the stains were not visible whilst wearing a jacket, and an orange tie, and his hair had been waxed and buffed and shone like a new pin. He looked a little nervous, and pulled at the bottom of his jacket to straighten it several times before his hostess arrived at the doorway. He offered the flowers and the two old people exchanged the usual forced courtesies before he was invited to cross the threshold and enter the communal hallway. Mrs Littleworth's door was wide open, and the hall was filled with the overwhelming aroma of old bacon, mildew, and unwashed armpits. My mother had heard the old woman vacuuming earlier in the day, so the importance of her visitor was unquestionable, for whilst the utilisation of a hoover may not be terribly out of the ordinary for most households, it was a rare event in the Littleworth one, as was the application of any form of cleaning fluid aside from thick disinfectant. Mrs Littleworth's residence was one where a thick coat of grease rendered kitchen work surfaces and cupboard fronts impenetrable to the most caustic of liquids and doubled up as an alternative to fly paper, and dust bunnies were house trained and kept as domesticated pets. As Mrs Littleworth flounced across the hallway with her gentleman caller, the scent of ten day old breakfast meat was joined by that of Devon Violets and Old Spice. And as the pair reached the entrance to the old lady's flat she turned to her visitor and spoke.

'Do come in Ben dear,' she said.

My mother recognised 'Ben dear' immediately as the old man who she had seen hanging around her building several times over the previous few weeks. And, moreover, she recognised his little red car as the same vehicle which had often been parked, during all hours of the day and night, opposite her living room windows, sometimes for a couple of hours or more at a time. She had never seen him in the car before, so had failed to make the connection, but after witnessing his exit from it that afternoon she began to realise that Guppy's presence in the vicinity of her flat was not a new development and she wondered, considering the amount of times she'd seen the red car in the vicinity while

Mrs Littleworth was away for a few days, if his relationship with the old lady was the only thing which had motivated his countless visits, and if perhaps Mrs Littleworth's treatment of her and Stella had been driven by more than petty rivalry and the onset of senile dementia.

As the possibilities began to sink in, I wondered why I had never considered them before. The Guppys and Floss Littleworth moved in the same circles, and by that I mean that they all fraternised with connivers and bigots who thought themselves above the common man and didn't have two brass farthings to rub together, and Floss Littleworth was apparently as regular a visitor to the deputy Mayor's dinner table as Pat Guppy claimed to be. They enjoyed the same pastimes, which were blackmail and threats of bodily harm followed by a copious amount of bin diving. And they shared a penchant for looking through keyholes and letterboxes, stealing mail, walking into people's homes uninvited, and sending poison pen letters.

During the days following that visit by Ben Guppy to Floss Littleworth's flat, the little red car took up its position opposite my mother's living room windows, at various times of the day or night, and remained there much as it had before for around two hours at a time. My mother had previously thought little of its appearance opposite her home, and had assumed that it belonged to a neighbour, or a visitor to the area who preferred to park in a local street and walk the remaining short distance into town, but the identification of its occupant had altered her perception of the significance of its presence, and she felt uneasy and, whilst she would not have wanted to admit it, a little threatened. She tried to conceal her concerns from Stella, Roy and myself, but it was inevitable that, as she had been aware of the Guppys' behaviour towards us over the previous years, and their part in Roy's assault, the threatening telephone calls we'd received, and the malicious letters that had been sent with the intent to intimidate us, she would begin to consider her own position as vulnerable. And as the little red car's visits increased in frequency and length, and the old man began to go out of his way to make his presence felt, she became more and more worried about her own safety and that of my sister.

As the end of August approached, the Guppys' car continued appearing across the road from my mother's flat, but the old man himself chose not to stay inside. Perhaps motivated by a certain amount of doubt that the connection between himself and Mrs Littleworth had been noted, he seemed to require some confirmation that his attentions towards my mother and sister were being appreciated. So he moved his point of observation from the safety of his car to a spot right outside Stella's bedroom window, and there he stood, sometimes for fifteen minutes at a time, examining the contents of the room from the limited view afforded through wooden slatted venetian blinds. And when I say that he took up a spot outside her window, I do not mean ten feet away, or five feet away for that matter. No. He positioned himself so close to the glass that, had it been winter and had the weather been cold enough, a mist would have appeared against the window when he exhaled. He made no effort to disguise his interest in both the room and its pretty young occupant, and it was only a matter of time before the hands he'd leaned against the sill to support himself, as he stood on tiptoes and pressed his nose against the glass to get a better look inside, gradually moved south into the depths of his front pockets.

When the old man was not hanging around my mother's place, grinning at windows or photographing them, or playing with himself behind a barely accommodating nearby bush or hedgerow, presumably because he was working a shift on our driveway instead, Floss Littleworth kept his place warm and carried out the tasks ordinarily allocated to him, aside from the manipulation of a pair of testicles as she did not have the necessary props, possibly in the belief that her efforts would be rewarded by an invitation from Pat Guppy to join some prestigious committee or other, and by prestigious I mean pretentious. She was far more conscientious than her male counterpart, and did not move from her allocated spot until a full ten minutes here or fifteen minutes there had been spent in constant surveillance. She carried a note book with her at all times, and anything noteworthy, such as my mother's departure from the building, the delivery of a parcel, the appearance of Stella to take in a supermarket delivery, the opening or drawing of curtains, or the wetting of a gatepost by Albert or Mush, my mother's dogs, was given a small pencilled entry in the old woman's written record of events. And when her time was up, and Ben Guppy appeared to take second watch, she would remain with him for the first five minutes to display recent additions to her notes and pass on any Polaroids she had taken.

Ben Guppy had a short attention span, as did his wife and Mrs Littleworth. So, not content with watching and photographing my mother's home and its inhabitants, including Mush and Albert, one or another of the elderly trouble-makers began making complaints to the environmental health department, about the state of my mother's flat, the emission of foul odours from it into the communal hallway, about the playing of loud music at all hours of the night and day, and to the RSPCA about her treatment of her dogs and the state of their health. And whilst the complaints were obviously, to any right minded person, merely malicious and petty, and were ultimately seen as such by the inspectors sent out to investigate the allegations, they still necessitated lengthy visits and numerous questions, and an invasion of my mother's privacy which she was sensible enough to suspect was only the beginning of things yet to come.

Indian take-away deliveries began arriving when unwanted, as did taxis and visits from window blind salesmen, and brochures for everything from hearing aids to surgical support stockings. Roofers turned up to issue quotations for repairs to her roof, plumbers for work to her bathroom, and builders for the extension she was apparently planning to her kitchen. Double glazing salesmen arrived armed with literature and testimonials, and Mr Worthing, the owner of a local carpet showroom not a stone's throw from my mother's front door, who had fitted her carpets just six months previously, arrived to offer an estimate for replacing the whole lot and laying wooden flooring. And then the telephone began ringing at all hours of the day and night.

There was, according to a very informative young gentleman in need of a second hand vacuum cleaner for a decent price, a card placed in the window of a local newsagent's shop which advertised such an item for sale. My mother was the one selling it, apparently, and her number was given for contact between the hours of half past eight in the morning and twelve o'clock at night. Moreover, she apparently had a washing machine and tumble dryer that she wanted to get rid of, and a number of small pieces of furniture. The side tables and magazine rack received little attention, although the same woman did ring up twice about the former, but the washing machine attracted numerous inquiries, from ladies both young and old, who thought the price was a little steep for such an old model but were willing to negotiate.

The Guppys had a flair for the ridiculous and absurd, so the arrival of the old pair one sunny afternoon at Floss Littleworth's front door, followed by the deposit of three deckchairs on the car park just outside her front windows, and the subsequent occupation of them by Ben Guppy, his wife, and his concubine, came as little surprise. Hot beverages and iced cakes were served half an hour after their arrival, with folded napkins and paper plates, and the tea and French Fancies were accompanied by a loud and lengthy discussion regarding the virtues of being an old person, far superior in intellect and social position, the inadequacies of all who had not yet reached the age of sixty, and the lessons which needed to be taught to the latter if they crossed the former. My mother, having heard of a similar performance in the vicinity of our home some time earlier, which had been attended by five times as many people, considered herself lucky that she was thought to merit the attendance of only three persons and, had all activities carried out in close proximity to her home have been similar in nature, she would most likely have chosen to turn a blind eye and go about her business as normal. But, as we had discovered over the previous three years, the Guppys were only ludicrous some of the time. For the remainder they were perfectly capable of causing distress and at times physical pain.

As Stella lay in bed one night at the beginning of September, having just turned out the lights as she prepared to go to sleep, she became aware of a small amount of movement outside her bedroom window and a tapping sound which was being emitted from the same place. She attempted to focus her attention on that spot and, as her eyes adjusted to the lack of light, made out the outline of a figure which had been picked out in silhouette by the light from the moon. Realising that her bedroom window had been left slightly open, to allow fresh air into the room, and that she had forgotten to put on the catch to prevent it from being opened fully, she watched as the light being reflected across the glass shifted, and the window began to move. Entirely paralysed for what seemed like an age, she watched in silence as the window opened to its full extent and the stranger placed his hand upon the inside sill as he prepared to lift himself up onto the ledge. Overcome by a feeling of complete helplessness and unable to locate anything which resembled a weapon with which to defend herself, she lay motionless under her covers as the dark figure climbed up onto the sill and prepared to enter the room. Movement near the foot of her bed and the sudden and quite overwhelming aroma of musty fur and beef Smackos brought Stella to her senses, and one swift blow with her heel to Albert's backside, sent the daft old dog flying from the bed, yapping and grumbling to himself and whoever had assaulted his rear end, and drove him off in the direction of the window and the intruder. Albert was as deaf as a post, partially sighted, and as daft as a brush, but his bark was a thousand times worse than his gummy bite and the sound of the big old spaniel barking from within the dark room sent the stranger toppling back off the ledge and onto the gravel below.

As the intruder had not forced the window open, or broken a lock, and he had stolen nothing as far as Stella or my mother were aware at the time, the policemen who arrived shortly after an emergency call was made explained that there was little they could do. Stella could not describe the intruder, as he had appeared as nothing more than a dark figure in an even darker room, and aside from a broken plant pot, which appeared to have broken the stranger's fall, there had been no damage to the property. Despite Stella's insistence that a check for fingerprints should at least be made, the two young police officers asserted that there was very little point, as the intruder had most likely worn gloves, and went on to say that even in the event that he had not worn protective coverings of some sort there was little chance that his prints would already be in the police database. Stella and my mother questioned, as I still do now, how the two policemen could possibly have arrived at such a conclusion, but Stella's continued requests that the matter be taken seriously were met with repeated references to the absence of forced entry, theft or assault, and some lengthy comment regarding the busy nature of police work and the responsibilities of home owners with regards to the closure of windows or doors and the fitting of adequate security. And then, with the obligatory lecture having been given, the officers informed my mother that the incident would be logged, which would apparently go no way in solving the crime but, when reports were released, would highlight the local force's failure in that respect, before departing in haste after having offered no assistance or reassurance.

The fact that we had chosen to resist every attempt by the Guppys to intimidate us, and had refused to give in to their blackmail threats, had resulted in three years of continual aggravation, but throughout that time we had been in control of our own destiny to the extent that the difficulties we encountered were partly determined by our own choices. No other person had taken the decision regarding whether to stand and fight or back down and give in away from us, and whilst it was ultimately the Guppys who were responsible for our anguish, we were conscious of the fact that its infliction was dependent solely on our willingness or unwillingness to comply with their demands. And our continued resistance had, up until that point, harmed nobody but ourselves. But all that had changed.

Perhaps the stranger had meant only to frighten Stella or my mother, and would not have ventured further into the room even if Albert hadn't chased him off, or maybe he had expected to find the room empty and had intended to steal a television set or dvd player to demonstrate his presence before escaping without ever having been detected. Who knows. But whatever his intentions, the mere fact that we could not know for certain what they had truly been inevitably resulted in lengthy discussions regarding the possible alternative outcome if Albert had not been present, or if my sister had gone to sleep earlier, or if my mother had been in the room and had attempted to prevent the intruder from entering. The possibilities were endless, and each one was more worrying than the next. The fixing of numerous window locks around the flat did little to allay my mother's fears, despite Stella's insistence, whether she believed it or not, that the stranger would most likely not return, and not one of us got very much sleep during the days which followed, as we lay awake wondering when the next incident would take place, and what form it would take.

As it turned out we didn't have long to wait. Just a week after the stranger's attempt to gain entry to Stella's room, a number of the flower pots and ornaments inside my mother's garden were smashed or stolen, and plants were ripped out from the soil and strewn around the ground beneath Stella's bedroom window. And if we were in any doubt as to the identity of those behind the theft, which of course we weren't as Ben Guppy had been joyfully skipping about the place during the days following the attempted entry into my sister's bedroom, the old man appeared on our driveway, wearing a very large grin and his Sunday best, holding one of my mother's garden ornaments in one hand and a bunch of withered geraniums in the other. He looked so completely pleased with himself, and so convinced that he had finally uncovered the route by which to attain his wildest dreams regarding our wealth and the distribution of it in his direction, that it was all I could do to prevent Roy from rushing out and flattening him.

'If you care about your family,' Pat Guppy called out from her doorway, as Roy returned home after helping my mother to erect a taller fence with an even stronger padlock, 'pay up or get out.'

She stood, feet spread apart and stomach bulging, with her arms crossed over her large breasts, which were barely contained within her body hugging black polo neck sweater, leaning back against the wall alongside her door for support. Her meaning was so blatant, her delight at having the upper hand was so evident, and her belief that the war was almost won could hardly be contained as she smirked and nodded in Roy's direction whilst repeating the remark in case it had not been fully appreciated the first time around. The old couple were so determined to make their point, and so fearful that we did not have the sense or intellect to understand their meaning, that they repeated similar comments several times over the following few days, and added suggestions regarding the safeguarding of my sister's virtue, the continuing good health of my mother, and the likelihood that one false move by us had the potential to ignite the spark that would burn my mother's flat to the ground or, worse still, leave its occupants as nothing but piles of ash. And all the time the little red car continued to make daily appearances opposite my mother's flat.

The notes which had been absent for some considerable time began arriving again, and one madly scrawled but carefully folded written composition arrived each and every evening from that point forward. At nine o'clock on the dot, the old man made his way up the steps to our flat as silently as was possible for a tumbling down fool who had once again taken to the bottle, and a little yellow slip of paper was pushed through our letterbox before he made his way back down the steps and collapsed on the drive in front of our car. Each note contained the same reference to previous bills which had remained unpaid and indicated the old pair's determination to issue proceedings through the small claims court, or to take some other form of action to recover the money, if the sum requested was not received by October 30th. The deadline was a new touch, and at least gave us some idea of the time scale we were looking at before the old pair would consider acting on their threats. And I did believe they had every intention of doing so. If we had previously harboured any doubts concerning the Guppys' willingness to go to extreme lengths to get what they wanted, their interest in my mother and sister, and the appearance of the intruder at the window of Stella's bedroom, had put pay to them once and for all.

The old man began turning up inside the communal hallway of my mother's building during the late hours of the evening, having been let in by Mrs Littleworth, who was always eager to oblige. And, along with the assistance of his sidekick, he pushed folded bits of newspaper under my mother's front door, calling out to her that next time he would put a match to them first. 'I'll burn you and yours, you whore' he'd shout, and he'd stay there for some time, sitting on the window sill opposite the entrance to my mother's flat, or standing right outside her front door with his face pressed against the glass, as he laughed aloud or called out, while his companion jumped up and down with excitement and urged him to continue as it was all such great fun. As he remained there for so long a time, Roy was often dispatched at speed, when he was at home and readily available, to see the old man off, and grabbing Ben Guppy by the collar before hurling him out onto his backside in the street did seem to quieten him down for a day or so. But the old man always returned, and it seemed inevitable that eventually it would not just be Ben Guppy who showed up at my mother's flat issuing threats but one of his hired thugs.

There were three options before us, which were namely to pay the old couple, leave our home, or kill one or both of the old buggers, although it did occur to me that the second of those possibilities would not necessarily have taken care of my mother's problem. We did not have the funds necessary to make the first two possible and were therefore left with only the third. Necessity is the mother of invention. Isn't that what they say? And drastic situations call for drastic measures. They say that too. So, ready or not, able or not, and in spite of some small continuing concern regarding the welfare of my immortal soul, I had no real choice but to have a good old think until I came up with a method, a time and a place, and the big pair of balls required to enable me to do the job. The method evaded me for quite some time, and therefore so did the time and place, and any balls I might have been able to locate appeared to have withered and dropped off, but what I lacked in those three areas I more than made up for in determination and motivation. Clueless and confused I might have been, but I'd never been more committed to anything in my entire life.

CHAPTER TWELVE

A SNIPER rifle, a good aim, and access to the roof of Tesco's supermarket would have afforded the cleanest way of dispatching the old man. But I did not own a gun, if I had I wouldn't have known how to load it let alone fire it, and in the absence of the first two things the third became obsolete. I doubted I had the stomach to drive a blade through the old man's heart, and imagined that particular organ would have been impossible to locate even if I could have held my lunch and summoned the strength to do the job. Hanging required a knowledge of knots which I did not possess, and battering was too messy. Strangulation, if carried out outdoors, took far too long and all those frustrated grunts and moans, most likely from me as much as my victim, were likely to attract attention before the task was completed. Drowning was difficult in the absence of a nearby stream or water butt, and I did not have the necessary long sword or axe required for a swift decapitation.

The average would-be assassin over complicates the whole business. Too many detective novels or television crime thrillers have left us all believing that crimes, especially those involving a homicide, have to be complex and clever, and we all give far too much credit to the detectives assigned to solving them. I suppose it is in the public interest to make fictional policemen, at least those of superior rank, intellectually superior to the criminals they seek, as I imagine that a constant display of good triumphing over evil must go some way in deterring members of the public from going beyond the law. But in reality there is no necessity for a murder to be convoluted and entertaining, like that contained within a two hour television drama, and the only real requirement, if the murder attempt is to be considered a success, is that the act results in the death of the intended victim and leaves no evidence to lead to the killer's arrest.

I simply required a method which did not involve the spilling of blood, or at least did not include me cleaning too much of the stuff up, was quick and silent, could be carried out without the assistance of an accomplice, and did not call for any great amount of bodily contact. I needed a location which was easily accessible by me, and one which the old man would willingly enter with very little encouragement or already frequented without any at all. The time of day depended upon the location, and the cost had to be minimal, as Roy would have noticed any sizeable withdrawal from our bank account. I was extremely aware of time ticking away, and doubted that it would be long before the old pair struck again. And so, with all of the above in mind, and following a great deal of thought and the formulation and subsequent abandonment of several highly imaginative schemes, I finally arrived at a solution and, in the interest of progressing with it, joined a local book group.

By the beginning of October the old man spent much of his time sitting in his car outside my mother's flat, and although he did still honour us with his presence every now and then, and continued taking photos, throwing stones, and shouting abuse at us if he had a moment to spare, the demands of his new occupation, and those of his increasingly unstable wife, meant that his routine was far more changeable than it had ever been before, and time spent in the vicinity of our flat was much reduced. There were only three events which occurred with any predictable regularity, and two of those took place during the afternoon. The first was his return to the building at half past twelve to make the old woman's lunch, which had been a daily occurrence for the previous ten or so years, according to Dave Roper. But he often brought with him one or another of the old couple's associates, and even when he returned home without invited company he regularly attracted the attention of passing school children who were of the opinion that he was a dirty old pervert and felt the need to express that for the entire street to hear, so he was seldom entirely alone. The second event happened only once a week, when the old man exited his flat at half past seven in the morning, on the dot, and travelled to the front of the drive, dressed in his pyjamas and carpet slippers, before dumping several Tesco's carrier bags filled with rubbish onto the pavement for collection and then returning to his flat and repeating the trip two more times. He was usually less than steady on his feet at that early hour, and looked as though he had hopped out of bed only moments before appearing on the drive, but the infrequency of this particular activity, and the fact that it was regularly witnessed by Mrs Palmer from next door, who appeared to time her rubbish disposal to coincide with that of her neighbour, made it an unattractive prospect when considering a time of day to bump the old man off. So, I had been left with only one viable option.

Mrs Gladys Wallis was eighty years old. I know that because she announced the fact when we first met, on the second Tuesday in October at eight o'clock in the evening. She was the eldest member of the book group, by about forty years, and had been the instigator of the meetings some twelve years previously.

The group had always consisted of between six and eight people, although the membership had changed over the years as old members had left and new ones had come aboard, and my joining created a little excitement as it took the group's number to nine for the very first time in its history. We met in Mrs Wallis' front room that first week, but the following meeting, I was informed, was to be in Mr Gibson's flat, and the one after that would be hosted by Alice Forman. My turn would come, I was told, but not until the fourth meeting on the 24th, by which time we should have finished Voltaire's 'Candide' and would be onto De Laclos' 'Dangerous Acquaintances', according to Mr Gibson, whose choice it had been. I took that as a propitious sign, considering the fact that I intended for Ben Guppy to make my acquaintance for the very last time that same evening, and to discover, albeit too late for it to do him any good, that I was nothing if not dangerous.

I had persuaded my mother to have a CCTV camera installed at the front of her flat, to deter the old man and any of his little helpers from entering her garden again. And, as with all things electronic or technological, she had some difficulty deciphering the instructions offered by the installer. So, arrangements were made for Roy to visit her on the 24th to ascertain the workings of the camera and offer suggestions for its most effective use. He was to arrive at around half past eight, and informed me that he would be around an hour, as he was planning to install some software on my sister's computer while he was there, to kill two birds with one stone.

And so, with my witnesses booked, and a plan in place to see Roy safely out of the way for a whole hour, I awaited the arrival of the 24th with a certain amount of anticipation. But it is the nature of the best laid plans that they invariably go wrong. I've no doubt that had my plan been ill conceived and doomed to failure, it would have gone ahead on the 24th, and that Ben Guppy might have survived, or I may well have been arrested immediately after killing him if I'd been successful, but his murder, or my failed attempt at it, would have taken place on the allocated evening at the allocated time. But as I had taken the trouble to come up with a fool-proof simple yet effective plan, a concrete alibi, and was assured that, even if my guilt was eventually uncovered, the police would have a darned hard time proving I was the culprit, and would suffer numerous headaches along the way, everything was undoubtedly bound to get knocked out of whack. Alice Forman was bound to come down with Chicken Pox at the age of thirty eight, being the only living soul within a fifty mile radius never to have had the disease as a child, and the date for my first stint at hostess to the book group was bound to be brought forward to the 17th, with the news of this alteration arriving just two days prior to that.

I could have taken that as a sign, couldn't I? That the old man should be spared. That I wasn't ready. That my plan was flawed. And I might have taken it as such and deferred killing the old man in order to reflect further, or decided to cancel the event altogether, had the next forty eight hours passed without incident. I might have considered it a second chance to find some alternative solution, if I'd been given a moment's peace. But no sooner had I put down the telephone receiver, after speaking to Mrs Wallis about the alteration to the venue for the meeting on the 17th, than a house brick found its way onto our bedroom carpet, having smashed through the window after being launched at it by Pat Guppy, and one brief glance from the window in the direction of the old woman and her husband, who had remained on the drive to survey the damage and congratulate themselves upon having caused us yet more expense and annoyance, left me reconciled to my fate, and to the old man's, and resolutely committed to ending my frustration and his life.

That evening saw the last ever gathering of elderly supporters on the drive attended by both Guppys. They did not know it then of course, as they talked loudly about revenge and imminent victory, and as they patted each other's backs and laughed at our expense, that there would never be another meeting like it. Each person present expressed their firm belief that the end was in sight and reassured the old man that he'd not have us for neighbours for much longer, but something told me that their glimpse into the future did not afford the same view as my own, despite the outcome being the same. With broken glass at my feet, and the cool evening air filling the room around me, I listened and watched as the old pair paraded and postured, and as their supporters pondered our imminent downfall and voiced their admiration for the malignant couple's resilience. One of the party asserted that a man who chose to go up against any one of their number was a damned fool, but that was met with stern looks from the old couple and raised eyebrows from everyone else, and the statement was summarily appended to indicate that the same man would be an even greater fool to go up against the Guppys who were an even greater force to be reckoned with than anyone else present. There was much jeering at the CCTV cameras, and at me too, as I assessed the damage to furniture near our bedroom window and collected small shards of glass from the sill. And as the group finally dispersed, the old woman called out to her departing comrades that she was looking forward to a much better Christmas that year, as the old man had promised her that she'd be facing a vastly improved New Year. I imagined the old man had made many such promises over the course of their marriage, he certainly had since we'd moved in, and I found myself wondering if he had ever kept a single one of them. Somehow I doubted it.

Roy thought my reaction to the broken window was a bit hard to fathom. He found my apparent lack of annoyance when recounting the evening's events, when he returned home from work, to be a bit confusing, considering the fact that we were about to fork out ninety pounds for the glass in our bedroom window to be replaced. In truth, I was angry, and had been for some considerable time, but I wore it well. He mistook my quiet readiness in preparation for the events of the 17th as a sign of resignation to our inevitable defeat, and asserted that he would not give in to the old pair as long as he continued to draw breath, implying that I might do otherwise. But the great difference between Roy and myself was that I could see a light at the end of the tunnel and was preparing for peace, but as all he saw was darkness, and an awful lot of it, he was preparing for a protracted period of all out war. There were moments when I wished I could have told him of my plans and eased his burden, but to be honest I considered the knowledge that I was about to commit murder might weigh more heavily than the prospect of a lifetime of Guppy madness.

Time slowed to such an extent during Ben Guppy's final two days on earth that I feared it would stop altogether. I had expected it to fly by, and had anticipated that at some point I would consider backing out as the deadline approached at too great a speed. To a certain extent I had felt that my humanity, or want of it, would be demonstrated by the existence of doubt and anxiety, or apparent lack of both. But there was no sudden hastening in the passage of time, no re-examination of my chosen course, and no desire to alter it. I wasn't calm so much as numb, as any feelings I had about the old man were transformed from sheer hatred to complete indifference. The anger I had experienced, and become accustomed to, was winding down. Hope replaced hatred, and I took that change to indicate that I had accepted there was no going back. The world seemed a far quieter place during those two days, and far less complicated. The events of the previous three years washed over me, and then faded. And while I would like to be able to say that I was in torment as I approached the time of Benjamin Arnold Guppy's demise, as that would imply that I was almost halfway human, in actual fact I thought little about him, and not at all about his wife.

And what of Ben Guppy? How did he spend his final forty eight hours on earth? Well, he spent most of the morning of the 16th observing the arrival of the glaziers who had been called in to repair our window frame, the fitting of a new pane of glass, and the subsequent departure of the fitters. He jeered at the men as they arrived, and frantically waved them off as they exited the drive on the way back to their van. He stood below the window, grinning from ear to ear, threatening to go off and locate another house brick, and then skipped back and forth along the drive, calling out to his wife to come and see the new glass, which he promised wouldn't be around for very long. He rushed, he paced, and he shouted an awful lot, although by that time the sound of his voice registered as nothing more than barely audible background noise which faded into silence as the day drew to a close. The pace of his life did not seem to have slowed at all, and I don't suppose there was any reason why it should have done, but the world had slowed around him and his hurried and erratic movements jarred with the space he occupied, as though the earth was already preparing for his removal.

I awoke at eight o'clock on the morning of the 17th, somewhat surprised that I had slept at all. I suppose I shouldn't have. I suppose I should have been beginning to experience a fraction of the guilt which I'd expected to engulf me before the day was out. But I felt nothing, aside from relief at finally reaching the big day after the longest forty eight hours of my life. I had not expected to look forward to the old man's death quite so much, although I'm not sure if it was the impending end of him so much as the end of waiting which ultimately gave me so much satisfaction. And to my great surprise, I was famished. I had never eaten breakfast in my entire life, as the mere thought of food before midday usually made me sick to my stomach, but by ten o'clock I had put away a bowl of cereal and two slices of toast, a large amount of tea and a glass of orange juice. Then, after collecting the post and examining its contents, I spent the remainder of the morning cleaning and vacuuming in preparation for the arrival of my reading companions. I did not feel nervous, I did not feel apprehensive, and any thought I did give to the evening to come was taken up with preparations for the group's arrival and the compilation of a shopping list, consisting mostly of bottles of wine and several kinds of fancy biscuits and cakes, as Roy had promised to go to the supermarket during the afternoon. It was probably terribly wrong of me to be thinking of chocolate cake at a time like that, but in truth I doubt that abstention from such thoughts would have gone any way in securing my soul's redemption, if indeed it needed to be redeemed. When you are about to commit murder there's little to be done to improve or worsen the situation, if you think about it. So Roy bought chocolate cake, and later that day I had two slices.

My mother had put up a certain amount of resistance when it came to having Roy over a week earlier than expected, as she'd planned to spend the evening with George Clooney and a box of chocolate mints. But I persuaded her that I was nervous about hosting the book group meeting for the first time, and that Roy's presence would make me even more so, and she'd been so pleased when I'd first joined the group, after worrying for three years that I seldom went out and socialised, that she agreed to make her CCTV camera available to him, to find enough jobs around the place to occupy him for at least an hour, and to put off soaking her feet in front of the television until the following night. So, as the time approached eight o'clock, and cars belonging to one or another member of the group began pulling up in the road alongside our home, Roy made his way out of our flat and headed off across town.

Gladys Wallis was the first to arrive, followed closely by Peter Gibson. Preliminary conversation was restricted to some discussion of the weather, as the storm predicted in local newspapers had begun to show signs of making an appearance after all, followed by comments regarding the state of local roads as my first two guests made their way into the hall and removed their coats. Gibson made his way into the living room, and if he did glance this way or that as he passed the bedroom and bathroom, to get some measure of his hostess' surroundings and by that some measure of her character, he did so without demonstrating it to anyone else present. Mrs Wallis was not so polite. She thought the number of pictures hanging on each wall, and she inspected each room to make sure, was excessive and bound to cause confusion or disorientation to anyone remaining within my home for longer than half an hour. She suggested some thinning out, and possibly the addition of a nice countryside scene. She was a bully, and I was in two minds, as she straightened the few pictures she did approve of and scrutinised the contents of my bookshelves, whether or not to tell her that I already had two just like her downstairs, and that I would soon only have one, so she should watch her step.

The inane chattering of my seven guests, as they discussed, disagreed, argued, and eventually agreed to differ, which was the inevitable outcome of any dialogue between them, was somewhat irritating. I contributed little during the first fifteen minutes, as those present ceased speaking so infrequently that I was almost entirely lacking in opportunities to take part. The following twenty minutes were dominated by Mrs Wallis, who would not be interrupted, and indicated as much in stern tones when sound was emitted from any quarter of the room not occupied by herself. The next ten minutes were quieter but equally uninspiring and, even if the time hadn't been ticking away and the imminent arrival of Ben Guppy hadn't been foremost in my mind, I had lost the will to participate. Everyone present required refreshment of one form or another, including Mrs Wallis who insisted she had not had more than a sip of red wine despite having finished half a bottle. So, as Mr Gibson took the floor, I took my leave and, with offers to assist me having been politely rejected, made my way into the hall and opened the cupboard which housed our CCTV monitor. The digital display told me that it was five minutes before nine, so I made my way to our front door, unlocked it, and engaged the catch. I walked from the small vestibule which housed the front door, closed the outer hall door behind me, and then made my way along the hall in the direction of my guests. A quick peek into the living room revealed little change in the seating arrangements of my visitors or the conversation taking place, and no indication that a trip to the bathroom by anyone present was imminent. So I confirmed that Mr Gibson required black coffee with two sugars, to demonstrate my continuing presence in the vicinity of the group, stepped into the kitchen momentarily to switch on the kettle, which had been filled with water earlier that evening, and then returned to the hall to await movement on the drive to appear on the CCTV monitor.

I heard the familiar sound of Ben Guppy's car door slamming shut just before nine o'clock. I'd become so familiar with every sound associated with the old couple, but that particular one was the most recognisable, apart from the slamming of their front door, and had followed or preceded almost every argument between the old pair during the previous three years. The old man, unable to inflict physical harm upon a passer-by or neighbour, usually for fear of being caught or punched on the nose, took out his frustration on inanimate objects, and his doors, both front and car, usually got the brunt of any violent outburst. It took the old man less than a minute to make his way from his car to our front door, despite stopping to examine several pieces of scrap wood put out by our neighbours earlier that day, as he made his usual visit to our letterbox with his little slip of yellow paper. And during those forty or so seconds I had opened the outer hall door, entered the small vestibule beyond it, closed the door behind me, put on a pair of surgical gloves, which Roy always kept in the house for the weekly toilet cleaning, and positioned myself behind the front door with my eye to the peep hole.

I watched as Ben Guppy began to ascend the twenty or so steps to our flat. He was grasping the usual piece of yellow paper in his right hand, and had foregone the use of the handrail as it was situated on his right side, just as he had done each night before, choosing instead to rely on the placement of one hand upon the square corner of the waist high stone wall to his left, which afforded little support and did nothing to prevent a fall. He climbed slowly, as though already out of breath, and his gaze was firmly fixed upon his feet as he made his way up to the front door in darkness. There was a light of course, but I had turned it off, and the old man had never discovered the switch at the foot of the steps, or the fact that it performed the same function of providing or removing light as the one I had flicked just moments earlier which was situated adjacent to the front door. He always paused just before he reached the top step. I had observed this element of his routine several times before from the same vantage point. And so, as he stopped for that brief moment, while he prepared to push that little slip of paper through the letterbox before him, I opened the front door and stepped forwards.

In truth there was little to do to force the old man backwards. The shock of my sudden appearance had done most of the work for me, coupled with his intoxicated state, and that had been a welcome surprise for me. The slightest application of pressure by both hands against the old man's chest finished the job, and as his facial expression travelled from shock to anger, and then reached its final resting place in fear, his feet lost any remaining claim they had on the concrete steps beneath him, his weight shifted backwards, and he began his descent.

I did not necessarily want to see Ben Guppy hit the ground, or several of the steps which led down to it. I would have preferred not to hear the anticipated crack as his head made contact with the concrete, or the snap as his neck broke. It was enough for me that I had killed him, I had no desire to gloat over the fact. But the CCTV camera at the front of the building, while it did not film the area directly in front of the front door, captured images from the lower section of the flight of steps the old man had climbed and subsequently toppled down, and as it was my intention to offer the tape as evidence to any police officer who called, I didn't want the sound of my front door closing to be picked up by the system. So I waited the thirty seconds necessary for the system to stop recording the event, which would undoubtedly have registered on the front camera's sensor, and then stepped inside, closed the front door, and quietly released the catch. I removed my gloves, opened the door to the hallway, closed the doors of the cabinet which housed the CCTV monitor, and made my way to the kitchen and the awaiting kettle which had not long boiled. I had been gone only three minutes at most, my guests were no further along in their discussion than they had been prior to my departure from the room, and not one of them had been alerted to the presence of the old man outside or my momentary exit from the flat.

Securing the good opinion of those investigating the murder you have carried out is not necessary, and goes no way in guaranteeing your freedom from prosecution. What have you lost if the detective sent out to catch the killer considers you to be guilty of the crime he is investigating if there is no evidence to support his suspicions? A great deal of effort expended in convincing the investigating officer that you are not guilty is a total waste of your time and energy, and will probably have an opposite effect to the one you desire, as policemen are trained to be suspicious of innocent looking people. At ease only in the presence of the guilty, as the police have such a great understanding of the criminal mind, too much innocence will make them uncomfortable, and will mark you out as the culprit. So, upon the arrival of Chief Inspector Woolly and his sergeant, Adam Paine, I did not feign sadness for the old man's loss or concern for his wife's bereavement. Gladys Wallis, although not acquainted with the old couple and therefore having nothing to gain or lose by Ben Guppy's sudden death, followed my example.

'Well, if a man his age will insist on climbing steps in the dark,' she said coldly, 'he must expect to fall down them.'

DS Paine's questioning of my guests, none of whom remembered taking a break much before quarter past nine, despite the fact that one had taken place fifteen minutes previously, resulted in the construction of a water-tight alibi for both myself and everyone else present. Mrs Wallis declared, when asked if anyone could have slipped away without being noticed, that not one person had done any furtive slipping, nor would they wish to when she was speaking, and insisted that all were present and accounted for at all times. At that point each member of the group, myself included, nodded in agreement. The presentation of the CCTV tape confirmed the time of the old man's death, and that he had been alone on the drive when it occurred. And the forensic examiner called in to ascertain the cause of death, though unwilling to give a definite answer before performing an autopsy, expressed his opinion that in all likelihood the old man had fallen to his death through nobody's fault but his own.

'Gawd, I can smell the whiskey from here,' DS Paine remarked, as he crouched beside the body and addressed the coroner. 'He must have been putting them away all night.'

Mrs Wallis rolled her eyes and tutted disapprovingly before going on to recount the story of her own father, a fall-down drunk, who had died in tragic circumstances some twenty years earlier.

'He was so inebriated,' she explained, 'that he fell asleep whilst eating a bowl of rice pudding and drowned in it.' The tears welled up behind her eyes. 'At least he died doing something he loved.'

As Ben Guppy's remains were carted off, his wife began shouting at the top of her voice, cursing God for allowing such a noble and good man to perish whilst the Devil, namely my husband, roamed the place as free as a bird.

'I'll be next,' the old woman called out to DS Paine, as he instructed the increasing number of onlookers to back away from the scene. 'You mark my words. I'll be murdered in my bed.'

At hearing the old woman's words, the crowd moved forward, ignoring the policeman's warnings to stay back, and several members suggested, as there was every likelihood that there'd be another murder in the vicinity before too long, that they shouldn't go home and risk missing it. The ever increasing number of onlookers added fuel to Pat Guppy's fire simply by being there, suggesting to the old woman that the strength in numbers was some indication of the strength of their affection. The flashing of camera bulbs, as the congregation immortalised the moment for their future grandchildren's consumption, confirmed that belief and inspired her to open her arms, in a movement suggestive of the prelude to a group hug, before expressing her gratitude to all assembled.

'You see,' she called out in my direction. 'You see how people around here care about my welfare. Would half as many turn out to see you murdered?!' She smiled in smug satisfaction before agreeing to go indoors with Mrs Palmer from next door.

The coroner's final verdict, after exploring Ben Guppy's innards, was that the old man had most likely lost his footing as a result of the huge amount of alcohol he'd consumed prior to attempting to climb the steps to the first floor; a conclusion which went no way in reassuring Pat Guppy that her life wasn't in danger, and failed to persuade her, much to Mrs Palmer's chagrin, that staying in her neighbour's spare room for any longer than a couple of weeks was unnecessary. Convinced that she was about to meet her maker, after having the life prematurely choked out of her, she refused to enter the driveway without a chaperone when she did return to pick up fresh clothes. After finally being cajoled into leaving Mrs Palmer's spare room, the old woman was shunted off to relatives, landing on the doorstep of one before heading off to another a couple of days later when she had outstayed her welcome. And then, alone and frightened, she finally made her way back to Hill View, where no reception committee gathered to greet her and no friendly neighbour called out to offer her a safe bed for the night. Forced to sleep in what she considered would soon be her deathbed, she lasted all of one night before succumbing to her fears and agreeing, with very little persuasion from Mr Axley, for whom an ample bosom and wrinkled stockings did not look so terribly alluring anymore, that

Tall Cedars retirement home should be her next stop. Defeated, and looking decidedly deflated, she exited the building one week later under heavy guard and was transported to the other side of town, where a single floral armchair in a communal sitting room awaited her presence.

Ben Guppy's funeral was a quiet affair, with only four mourners in attendance according to Dave Roper, who was one of them. His wake, which was held at Mr Axley's residence, promised to be an altogether more lively event as every neighbour, plus a distant cousin or three, arrived to partake of the promised buffet and selection of wines and beers, but ended abruptly when refreshments ran out. My interest did not lie in either event.

As soon as the grave was covered over and a headstone had been firmly fixed in place, and following a trip to the local supermarket to pick up a bottle of decent cabernet sauvignon, I made my way to the cemetery which had become the old man's new home, and took out a corkscrew and a large globular wineglass. Emptying the contents of the bottle until the glass was full to brimming, I raised the latter above my head and suggested to the residents of nearby plots, who were less than enthusiastic, that they join me in toasting the absence of Ben Guppy. The sound of five or six bright red party poppers exploding filled the air, as strings of curly pink, yellow and blue tissue paper danced on the breeze before landing on the soft grassy ground at my feet. And then, after finishing off the glass of wine and taking a deep breath to ready myself, I began to sing. I skipped, hopped and jigged, as I moved around the old man's grave, and then twirled and flounced as I crossed in front of the stone marker which displayed his name. As the sun disappeared behind a distant hill and the light faded away, I paused to refill my glass. I smiled, taking a moment to contemplate the peace and quiet which had already begun to engulf my home and family since the old pair's departure, and then raised my glass one last time, in celebration of the wonderful demise of an incredibly irritating old man.

Printed in the United Kingdom by
Lightning Source UK Ltd., Milton Keynes
137312UK00001B/196-204/P